aLex uNLimiteD

THE VOSARAK CODE

AUTHOR	Dan Jolley
EDITORS	Paul Morrissey
	Kara Stambach
LAYOUT ARTIST	Jennifer Carbajal
COVER DESIGNERS	Anne Marie Horne
	& Al-Insan Lashley
INTERIOR ILLUSTRATIONS	Jared Boone
PRE-PRESS SUPERVISOR	Erika Terriquez
ART DIRECTOR	Anne Marie Horne
DIGITAL IMAGING MANAGER	Chris Buford
PRODUCTION MANAGER	Elisabeth Brizzi
MANAGING EDITOR	Vy Nguyen
EDITOR-IN-CHIEF	Rob Tokar
VP OF PRODUCTION	Ron Klamert
PUBLISHER	Mike Kiley
PRESIDENT AND C.O.O.	John Parker
C.E.O. & CHIEF CREATIVE OFFICER	Stuart Levy

First TOKYOPOP printing: May 2007

10 9 8 7 6 5 4 3 2 1

Printed in the USA

ALEX UNLIMITED: The Vosarak Code.
© 2007 Dan Jolley and TOKYOPOP Inc.
"Alex Unlimited" is a trademark of TOKYOPOP Inc.

Library of Congress Cataloging-in-Publication Data

Jolley, Dan.
  Alex unlimited : the Vosarak code / written by Dan Jolley.
    p. cm.
  Summary: Able to summon parallel-dimension versions of herself equipped to handle any task, eighteen-year-old Alex Benno, herself a plain and very average girl, resents these idealized women and the fact that she never gets any credit for the spectacular feats they accomplish while working for a secret government spy agency.

  ISBN 978-1-4278-01227
  [1. Spies--Fiction. 2. Espionage--Fiction. 3. Self-confidence--Fiction. 4. Science fiction.] I. Title.
  PZ7.J66244Ale 2007
  [Fic]--dc22

                                        2006033981

chapter one

"I realize how hard this must be, Jacob," said Claudia, the woman code-named *Alex Prime*. She adjusted her cell phone headset, kicked the man before her in the jaw, then continued, "but I really think we need to talk about your mother."

The man thudded limply to the floor. The remaining four gunrunners—who would go into the report as Huey, Louie, Stewie, and Screwy, and the Bureau could figure out their real names—edged closer to her.

A voice wailed through the phone, "My *mother?* I'm not talking to you about my mother! I don't even know you!"

Huey raised a crowbar. Claudia darted forward and punched the point of his chin. He dropped to the floor. The remaining three men glared at her, not moving. Not yet.

She pivoted, watching them carefully. "That's no problem, Jacob. My name is—" She caught herself, but covered for it smoothly. "Call me Claudia."

The criminals, some unconscious, were alone with her in the laundry room of a fourth-rate hotel in Rio de Janeiro, Brazil. Outside, the city bustled and hummed, alive with late-night energy. Everyone out there was completely unaware of the drama unfolding inside.

Well, almost everyone. The people in the windowless van parked down the street knew *exactly* what was going on.

From the phone: "Claudia . . . ? That your real name?"

"Yes, it is. And I'm serious about your mother, Jacob. You know full well she wouldn't approve of what you're doing."

She narrowed her eyes at Stewie, who'd taken a step forward. He paused, thinking better of it.

On the other side of several thick walls, an American named Jacob Lindsay crouched inside the hotel's main office. He was a small, rodent-like man, with eyes that darted about nervously, rapidly blinking away sweat. He held a phone in one trembling hand and a gun in the other.

The hotel's manager, a Brazilian woman in her early thirties, sat on the floor, frozen stiff. She stared down the barrel of Jacob's gun.

"You don't know anything about my mother!" Jacob shouted into the phone. He sounded very close to snapping. "She doesn't care what happens to me!"

"I think she does," Claudia answered. "I think she'd know that you didn't *really* mean to get involved. Not this deeply. She would understand that you're in over your head, and you're afraid you'll never be able to find your way out now."

Apparently still irritated that Claudia had forcibly disarmed them all within seconds of her arrival, Louie decided to rush her, screaming, "Grab her legs! If she can't stand up, she can't fight!"

Claudia had no choice but to tag him a couple of times—once with a knee, once with an elbow. She eyed the two that remained standing. "You realize I'm trying *not* to hurt any of you, right?"

In the office, his eyebrows squeezed together, Jacob said, "Huh? What's going on? Are my guys still out there?"

"Nothing's going on," Claudia answered quickly. "Tell me, Jacob . . . how could you say your mother doesn't care? She gave birth to you, didn't she? Raised you, all by herself?"

A few seconds ticked by. Jacob's breath grew more ragged . . . and then he made a tortured sound into the phone, something like a whimper. His voice came out small. "How'd you know she raised me on her own?"

"Just a guess," Claudia said. "Jacob . . . don't you think she's at home right now, hoping, even *praying*, that you're all right?" She raised a warning finger at Screwy. "Don't you think it would break her heart to see you like this? Wouldn't it just kill her to know you had the chance to make all this right, and didn't take it?"

Claudia heard Jacob start to sob. It took several more seconds, but he finally said, "Yeah. Yeah, it . . . I guess it would."

Two blocks down and across the street from the hotel (a distance determined to pose no threat), Alexandra Benno was in the back of the windowless gray van, sitting across from two armed men wearing boring gray suits. Claudia's conversation with Jacob Lindsay played through earpieces they all wore; her voice was rich and soothing despite the circumstances.

"She's a real spitfire, isn't she?" said one of the men in gray suits.

Alex slumped in her seat and rolled her eyes.

Back in the laundry room, Claudia spoke into the phone. "I knew you'd realize it eventually, Jacob. You're not alone. You've still got someone who loves you, who wants you to be safe."

She took a moment while the last two men attempted to do what their cohorts couldn't; charging in, they knocked her off balance and tried to dog pile on top of her. This resulted in a chaotic tangle of arms and legs, followed by several sharp cracking sounds.

Claudia shoved the unconscious thugs off her and got back to her feet. With an extra note of understanding in the tone of her voice, she said, "I'd like to come back to the office and talk with you, Jacob. Do you think that'd be okay?" She paused for a carefully measured three seconds. "Don't you think that's what your mother would want? So she could see you again?"

In the office, Jacob Lindsay wavered, uncertain . . . and then carefully, deliberately, he set the gun on the floor.

"Sure," Jacob murmured, defeated. "Sure. Come on."

The hotel manager practically collapsed with relief.

In the van, one of the gray-suited men pulled out a satellite phone and hit a button. After a few moments, he said, "She's done it, sir. We'll have the location of that arms shipment in no time." He listened briefly. "No, sir. No loss of life at all."

Alex watched as the two agents allowed themselves brief grins. She scowled and slumped down even farther.

* * *

The ride back to the airport was as excruciating as usual. The van rumbled along, all four heavily armored tons of it. Alex stared bitterly at the floor. Brazil was the twenty-third country she'd been to. *Twenty-third.* And the only sights she ever got to see were boring hotel rooms and the insides of vans just like this one.

Muffled laughter reached her from the front seat, barely audible through the steel plating. Of course Claudia got to sit up there with the driver, enjoying the *view,* while she had to stay back where it was *safe.*

Alex caught herself. *Dammit, don't be so childish.* She conscientiously sat up straighter.

"So, what do they do, give you a private tutor or something?" The question from the agent who'd referred to Claudia as a "spitfire" caught Alex off guard. She thought his name was Stimes; he was new. The other agent was on the phone again, not listening.

"I'm not in school anymore," Alex replied, then thought for a second about how strange those words still sounded.

"Not in school?" Stimes frowned, uncomprehending. "You can't be more than fourteen, can you? Fifteen, tops."

Ugh. Pained, Alex started fidgeting with her hair. "I turned eighteen two weeks ago."

Stimes said, "You're serious? Well."

And then he gave her the quickest glance-over. A tenth of a second at most, but right from her head down to her feet—and even though he didn't say anything else, Alex understood him perfectly: *I'm sure you'll start to blossom any day now.*

Alex didn't look at or talk to Stimes for the rest of the trip. She didn't trust herself to speak anyway; his "appraisal" had made her feel so rotten and hopeless. She did spend several hours during the drive entertaining a fantasy in which she complained to the right people, including the Bureau Chief himself, and got Stimes fired on the spot.

She knew nothing like that would actually happen.

But it was fun to think about it, at least.

* * *

The Bureau of General Operations had, ironically, only one specific mission: working with people like Alex Benno. The BGO occupied a massive, perfectly cube-shaped, red-brick building (commonly referred to as "the Square") on an unremarkable street in Washington, D.C. From the outside it looked plain, even a little run-down; it was the kind of place that could house virtually any business, from a daily newspaper to an auto parts store.

For sixteen of her eighteen years Alex Benno had called the Square home. Until two weeks ago, of course.

Since they were back in the States and on what the Bureau considered secure ground, Alex was allowed to ride in a standard-issue car rather than the hulking armored vans where she sat during the field work. She was grateful to be able to sit in the back seat, gaze out the windows, and take in the world around her. She just wished it didn't take so much effort to ignore the conversation *inside* the car, where Claudia-in-the-front-seat had Agent Stimes wrapped tightly around her little finger.

God, how gross. Stimes had to be at least forty.

Of course, Alex Prime looked to be in her late twenties this time. Maybe that wasn't so bad.

But still. *Ecchh.*

"So you're in, I mean to say, you actually work in Hollywood? In the movies?" Stimes was quite eager to continue chatting with Claudia.

Claudia ran one hand over her hair—a more elegant version of the gesture Alex often unconsciously made—and smiled. "Consulting work, yes. I did some modeling before I went to med school, so I still had contacts in the entertainment industry. It wasn't that difficult a transition."

"Huh . . . so you make sure the doctors in the movies get things right, then."

"Sometimes I do medical consulting, yes, but it's mostly psychological material they want me for. That's my specialty."

"Psychology?"

"Mm-hmm. Primarily *male* psychology."

Claudia lowered her eyelids ever so slightly. The movement simultaneously accentuated her eyelashes and made Alex want to gag. There was shameless flirting, and then there was whatever *this* was.

Alex did her best to tune out the rest of what Stimes and Claudia had to say until the huge, familiar sight of the Square came into view.

chapter two

As usual, the crowd thronged around Claudia as soon as she walked into the room. Several of the guys couldn't stop applauding as they surrounded her; it made for some awkward attempts at handshakes, but Claudia was gracious about it.

She always was.

"Oh my God, the way you disarmed those thugs, it was like watching a ballet!"

That was Bob from Research & Development. His eyes kept dancing between Claudia's movie-star face and her perfect figure. She acted as if she didn't notice.

"Well, Bob," Claudia gushed, "I couldn't have done any of that if I hadn't had you guys backing me up."

Bob grinned an absurdly wide grin.

The party was in the south conference room—the usual place, since it had the big set of double doors best suited for the Primes' grand entrances. Alex slipped in through a side door, skirting the festivities in the center. She knew no one would pay her any attention, but she tried to force her messy curls back up into their bun anyway.

Approaching the table with the punch bowl on it, Alex saw Matthew from Damage Control push through the crowd with his trademark cocky swagger, eager for some face-to-face time with Claudia.

"I just wanted to tell you how much we all enjoyed working with you," Matthew said in that slick way he had. "We were patched in through the R&D's button-cam, and *man*, that elbow you landed on the guy's collarbone! What was *that?*"

"Snow Tiger Kung-Fu," Claudia purred.

Matthew looked smitten. "Well, like I was saying before, this has been great. I think you're the best one we've ever had, honestly."

Claudia laughed a little at that—a small, perfect sound, like the chime created when two fine crystal goblets clinked together.

Standing at the punch bowl with a sweating glass of ginger ale in her hand, Alex rolled her eyes. She'd been mouthing Matthew's lines along with him.

But she focused mainly on Claudia.

Alex hated these "going away" parties even more than she hated the invitations that got the whole thing started in the first place. Claudia, or whoever, was always mobbed by every guy in the BGO, always standing there like a damn supermodel, with her skin, and her hair, and did Claudia's waist *have* to be that tiny?

She knew what people saw when she and the Alex Prime du jour stood beside each other. Alex, short and scrawny, with hopeless hair and the figure of a twelve-year-old boy . . . next to an older woman (usually) who pretty much got it right in every way that Alex had it wrong.

When men described Alex Prime, the adjectives ran to the excessive. Genius. Stunning. Artistic, usually. Luscious, always.

Alex herself had to settle for a less impressive list. Average. Mediocre. Plain. Over and over again, every *single* time, you'd think that at least *once* Alex wouldn't look and feel quite so bad by comparison.

It hadn't happened yet.

Before Alex's train of catty thoughts gained any more momentum, she noticed Matthew break away from the crowd and head straight for her. He was really walking toward the punch bowl, of course, not her, and she knew that, but at this point it would look awkward if she just walked away. Plus, for those three or four seconds . . . she held onto the hope that he might actually be coming to talk to *her*.

Alex desperately ran a hand over her frizzy curls, then took a sip of the ginger ale. She prayed he wouldn't notice her glass shaking.

"Hey, Alex," Matthew said, in the tone that she knew meant *Hey, Alex. I'm being polite to you because it's expected of me.*

"Matthew." She winced as her voice did that nervous thing that made it go up an octave on the last syllable.

He filled two glasses with punch. "She's really something, isn't she? Talking the guy into giving himself up like that?"

Not trusting herself with any more actual words, Alex simply squeaked.

"Well, anyway . . ." He turned to go. "You're part of a great team, kid. You should be proud of her."

"Oh, I am," Alex said, because she couldn't think of anything else to say, but he was already swaggering away.

Grimacing, Alex dumped the rest of her drink onto a ficus tree, glared at the mass of people congratulating and flirting with Claudia, and slunk out of the room.

The hallway gave her some welcome quiet. She pressed her back against a wall and slid down to sit on the floor, her eyes closed.

The peaceful respite didn't last long.

"You know, you'll give yourself early wrinkles if you keep frowning that much."

Alex looked up at Second-in-Command, who'd miraculously materialized a few feet away. For someone who talked as much as Sec did, she carried herself with annoying silence.

Second-in-Command, if rumors were to be believed, had yet to see her thirtieth birthday; no one would know it to look at her, though, since she dressed like the sternest of stern librarians. The very dark skin on her face was free of worry lines, but with the granny glasses and the utilitarian hairstyle, she could have easily passed for forty.

Sec had a briefcase tucked under one arm as she absently riffled through a stack of papers with both hands. Her glasses threatened to slide right off the tip of her nose.

Alex sighed. "Is it time to send her back yet?" she asked, trying not to sound too hopeful.

Sec made a mildly disapproving sound with her tongue. "It's Prime's moment of glory, Alex. No need to rush it."

Alex couldn't help groaning. "*Moment* of glory? She's had *ten whole days* of glory."

Sec looked up from her papers. "I'm sorry?"

Alex stood and scowled at Sec. "Oh, are you *kidding* me? Alex Prime this, Alex Prime that. Why does *she* get to be 'Alex Prime' anyway? *I'm* the one that makes it all happen! If anybody should be Alex freaking Prime, it should be *me*. Shouldn't it?"

Sec's eyes had widened; she was taken aback as Alex spoke. Now she tried to shift her papers around, covering for the sudden, awkward silence, but instead she accidentally scattered them all over the floor.

Alex looked at the heap of papers, wishing she could pull every word she'd just said back out of the air, *knowing* she'd acted in the exact ways she shouldn't: whiny, immature, and selfish.

"Um," Sec began, crouching down, "could you give me a hand with these? Please?"

Alex mumbled an apology and kneeled to help Sec.

They had just gathered up the last of the papers when the conference room's side door opened. Claudia walked out, smiling and waving goodbye to someone still inside, then noticed Alex and Sec. She flashed them a friendly smile and said, "Need a hand?"

Polite as always. *Helpful* as always. Alex often found herself wishing Code-Name Alex Prime could be completely evil and despicable, just *once*, so she could hate her with a clear conscience. That never happened, of course. Alex Prime (despite her scathing condescension, or unpredictable flares of temper, or pathological flirtatiousness, or whatever unpleasant trait she might show up with) was a good woman. That's why she was summoned in the first place.

"No, I think we've got it," Sec answered. She glanced down the hallway. "Just about time to go, I believe. Are you ready?"

"Sure." Claudia's smile widened. "This has been great, and of course I'm happy to help and all, but it *will* be nice to get home."

"Follow me, then." Sec moved down the hallway, with Claudia in tow. Sec looked over her shoulder and said, "Alex? Coming too?"

It wasn't really a question.

The three women made their way deep into the proverbial bowels of the building, taking an elevator to the sixth floor below street level.

As the elevator's machinery hummed, Claudia peered down at Alex. "We never really got a chance to talk, did we? Not after that first day."

Alex shrugged. "Sometimes that's the way it happens."

"I'm sorry about that," Claudia said. She sounded as if she might actually mean it. "I guess I got caught up in the whole . . . *adventure* of it, y'know?"

Alex shrugged again. That was just lip service. She figured if Claudia had really wanted to talk to her, she'd had ample opportunity. Claudia might have said more, but the elevator came to a halt and the doors opened.

"Come along, please." Sec led the way down a short corridor to a thick metal door. She punched a lengthy code into a keypad set in the wall; several locks *thunked* open, and the metal door slid aside. Sec led the way into a lab area, a sort of rabbit warren of sterile, interconnected rooms stocked with scientific equipment.

"Do we need to go back into that first room for this?" Claudia asked, looking around calmly.

"No," Sec replied. "This area is secure enough. The return trip doesn't need as much handling."

"All right, then." Claudia turned to Alex and, surprisingly, reached out and took one of Alex's hands in both of hers. "Maybe next time we can hang out a little more."

Alex hesitated. A few sarcastic remarks sprang to mind, but she decided against them. Suddenly she felt tired and just wanted to get it over with. "Sorry. I don't think there's going to be a next time."

Claudia let go of Alex's hand and gave a little nod of understanding. "Well. Okay. Whenever you're ready."

Alex nodded, then closed her eyes and bowed her head in concentration.

The air around Claudia began to change, distort, like summer's heat waves on blacktop . . . and the woman code-named Alex Prime *vanished* in a sparkling, shimmering cloud of lights.

Alex and Sec were left alone in the lab as the last of the glistening motes faded out. "I'm pretty tired," Alex said. "You need me for anything else?"

All business, Sec said, "No, that's it for today."

Alex nodded. "Cool. I'm going home."

* * *

In his office on the second floor, Matthew Voltz, the object of Alex's infatuation (and derision), closed his door and quietly locked it. When he walked to his desk the overconfident strut was gone. Instead, he moved like someone on the brink of exhaustion. He sat down heavily, tried to steady his breathing, then pulled a 35-millimeter film canister from his pants pocket and pried the rubberized lid off with one thumbnail.

Matthew had picked up the canister from a dead drop—a pre-designated, inconspicuous place where someone else could leave messages for him to retrieve at a later time. That way the sender and receiver never had to be seen together; it was a classic espionage technique. Matthew stared down at the canister with undiluted hatred as he pulled out the tiny scroll from inside it.

On the paper, printed on a kind of LaserJet that could be found in thousands of copy centers across the country, was a very simple note:

SAME DEAL AS BEFORE

YOU HAVE TWO DAYS

Matthew crumpled up the paper and dropped it into the ashtray on the edge of his desk. He pulled a lighter out of another pocket and set the note on fire, watching with a stony expression as the message quickly turned to ash.

chapter three

Alex drove her humble little car out of the BGO parking garage. The attendant hit the button to raise the gate, but as usual he didn't speak. *No reason why he should*, Alex thought glumly.

It was about 2:30 in the afternoon—a bright, warm, late-summer day with only a few wispy clouds in the sky. Traffic sucked, but that was nothing new, not in D.C. At least she didn't have far to go: out of one parking garage, five blocks over, and into another garage at the Ash Tree Condominiums. She left her car in its reserved space and rode up to the ninth floor.

Two weeks. That was how long Alex had been a legal adult. Two weeks ago she turned eighteen. Her friends Gail and Chuck threw her a pitifully tiny but very sweet party, and Sec gave her the keys to this place.

"As long as you're sure," Sec had said.

Of *course* she was sure. She certainly didn't want to live the rest of her life in the BGO dormitory where she and a couple dozen other children had been raised.

Walking into the condo, though, she didn't feel much like an adult. Despite having her own kitchen, living room, bedroom, and even a second bedroom that she could call her "office" (all of it in spacious contrast to the cramped twin-bed dorm room), the only thing she felt was intense loneliness.

Well, she was alone but *not* alone, in a couple of different ways.

A brash voice croaked out, "Alex! Alex! Best friends! Alex!"

Perched in a cage near her balcony's sliding doors was a large green parrot. She raised an eyebrow at the bird and walked over to it. "Hi, Worsel. Did you miss me?"

"Alex! Best friends! Alex!"

The parrot was the Bureau Chief's idea, not Alex's. He'd come with the condo, along with a pamphlet about his proper care and feeding.

Because she *wanted* a big, weird, loud bird to live with her.

She knew he'd been fed and tended to in her absence. That was the other "not alone" part. She went away? Someone took care of her things. She broke down on the side of the road? You'd better believe someone showed up with a tow truck in five minutes flat. Someone, someone, someone— there was *always* someone. Even on the drive from the Square to her condo, she knew someone had kept an eye on her the whole way.

She didn't know any of them. Never really saw any of them. But she knew they were there. It was never in question.

Alex turned and surveyed the rest of her place: the tiny breakfast table, really only big enough for one person. The recliner in front of the TV—again, suited for one since there was no couch yet. Her bedroom held the place's only real luxury: a big, comfortable four-poster queen-size bed . . . in which, of course, only one person had ever slept.

"Y'know, Worsel, when I asked for all this, I thought I'd enjoy it."

The parrot said, "Dinner time! Dinner time!"

Alex chuckled humorlessly and went to get the bird food.

A few minutes later, after Alex had determined that there was nothing of interest on TV, that she had read every book and magazine there, and that it might be a little excessive to start over on her DVD box set of *Quartz Princess* for the nineteenth time, she picked up the phone and dialed a number that very few people knew. It rang twice, then a bright, highly energetic voice answered, "Hi!"

Gail Shikari. She always answered the phone like that—as if she already knew who it was, caller ID or not. She talked to everyone as if they were her dearest friend in the whole world. Of course, Alex liked to think she *was* Gail's dearest friend in the whole world. One of two, anyway.

A photograph of Alex, Gail, and Chuck hung on the living room wall near the kitchen, the three of them posing in the dorm room that Alex and Gail used to share. In the photo,

Gail's chin came to just above Alex's eyebrows, and her short, spiky black hair looked especially turbulent, highlighting her sparkling grin.

"Chuck" Houston—Chuck being short for Charlotte—came off a little more demure, as usual, with her long blonde hair partially covering one eye.

"It's me," Alex said into the receiver.

"Alex! Hi! Where are you?"

"Here at the new place. What're you guys doing?"

"Studying," Gail replied, her energy dipping a bit. School was just now back in session. "Got our first round of tests coming up. *God*, I envy you, being out of all this!"

Alex glanced around the living room. Worsel squawked at her. "Yeah, I'm living the life. Is Chuck there?"

"Yeah, want to say hi?"

"Sure."

The phone made that rustling sound that phones do when they get handed from one person to another, and then a different voice came through: "Benno! What's goin' on with ya?"

Alex couldn't help giggling. She and Gail and Chuck had all been raised together in what amounted to an exceptionally high-quality state orphanage where they were nurtured and educated by painstakingly selected caregivers and teachers. They had received what most people would consider an extremely solid, perhaps even classical education.

But something the BGO did *not* do was provide its charges with street knowledge. Alex's contemporaries were all intelligent, reasonably well-adjusted people, but they weren't exactly cool.

Chuck heard Alex giggle and she said, "Hey, no mocking of the hip vernacular!"

That made Alex laugh even harder. "Hi, Chuck. They've already got you cramming, huh?"

"Ah, you know how it is, Benno. Same ol' same ol.'" She dropped the affectation. "When are you going to have us over again?"

Alex kicked back in her recliner. "Funny you should ask. I was thinking tonight—I could pick you both up, maybe rent some movies, order a pizza."

"Oh, hey, sorry, not tonight. This Anatomy & Physiology test is going to kill us unless we get all this stuff nailed down. Maybe Friday?"

Alex frowned. It was Tuesday. "Um. Yeah . . . yeah, Friday would work."

"Okay, good, it's a date!"

"Great. Well, hey, I know you two are busy and all. I'll call you again maybe Thursday night, okay?"

"Sounds good. Talk to you then."

Alex hit the "off" button on the phone, got out of the recliner, and slowly walked over to an official *Quartz Princess* dartboard affixed to the living room's far wall, opposite where Worsel's cage stood. She glared at the bull's-eye for a few seconds, then pulled the five darts out of their rack (each of them cast to resemble the show's streamlined battle cruiser, the *Great Bear*) and walked to the line of masking tape she'd set down on the floor to mark the proper distance.

Carefully, carefully, she aimed the first dart, then let it fly.

Thunk.

Claudia and her flirting and her tight clothes.

Thunk.

Stimes in the van and his insulting little once-over.

Thunk.

Stupid Matthew and the lines he used every *single* time.

Thunk.

"As long as you're sure this is what you want."

Thunk.

Alex started to frown as she walked back to the dartboard, and it grew deeper the closer she got. Not one of the darts had come even *close* to the bull's-eye, and two of them had missed the board entirely and now stuck out of the wall. *Oh well. Guess that'll come out of the Bureau's security deposit.*

Suddenly the excuse she'd given to Sec earlier seemed very true: Alex was tired. *So* tired. She went in the bedroom, pulled off her jeans, turned back the huge down-filled comforter on the bed, and crawled in.

She was asleep in under two minutes.

chapter four

At that moment, several thousand miles to the east, thunder rumbled across a low charcoal-gray sky. A sleek, exquisite, convertible sports car rocketed along a narrow lane, zipping through the Italian countryside moments ahead of the storm.

The car's driver, Sabre Cromwell, looked to be in his late thirties, a lean, slender whippet of a man with salt-and-pepper hair and a cruel, perfect smile. Lightning flashed overhead and he laughed, reveling in the thunder that followed.

Cromwell took a sharp right onto an even narrower lane and followed it more than a mile, speeding around its many twists and turns, until he came around a small hill . . .

The Manor spread out before him. He didn't know how many rooms this place had. He'd never bothered trying to count. But he did know that this ancestral home was bigger than the hospital where his mother had scrubbed floors when he was a boy.

Cromwell respected the wealth that the Manor represented, but he respected its owner's power even more.

When he screeched to a stop at the base of the wide marble stairs leading up to the Manor's grand front entrance, a butler came out to meet him. Cromwell leapt from the car. He looked like an Olympic gymnast.

"Will you be staying long, sir?" the butler asked in faintly Italian-accented English.

Cromwell answered him with what could pass for an Australian twang. "Don't know. Keep the car handy, would you?"

The butler started to say, "Of course, sir," but was interrupted. He and Cromwell both turned at the sound of rapidly approaching helicopter blades.

As they watched, a large luxurious helicopter descended from the clouds. Cromwell chuckled at the pilot's nerve, flying in this weather, but he wasn't surprised given the identity of the passenger.

The helicopter landed on the Manor's vast front lawn; one of the chopper's doors opened, and the most beautiful woman in the world stepped out.

That was how Cromwell always thought of Sonnet Ivandrova. Even though he could never be sure how much of her beauty was real and how much was illusion, it didn't matter; she touched his heart more profoundly than the finest masterpieces of chiseled marble or oil on canvas. He could never get enough of her.

"Sabre," she said as she approached him. "Do you know why we're here?" Her words flowed out in a tantalizing mixture of British and Russian inflections.

He shook his head. "Obviously the old man thinks it's important."

Sonnet nodded once—a subtle, flawless movement—and Cromwell offered her his arm, which she took with her typical grace. The two of them climbed the rest of the stairs and entered the Manor.

The mansion's interior was every bit as opulent as its exterior, replete with glossy black marble floors and accents in twenty-four-karat gold. Sabre Cromwell and Sonnet Ivandrova made their way through the wide entrance hall and up a grand staircase, where they approached a single door at the stair's head.

The door stood ajar. As soon as their feet left the top step, a voice came to them from inside—a voice so deep and coarse it sounded like a gigantic engine revving.

"Thank you both for joining me."

Cromwell held the door open for Sonnet, then followed her in.

They entered a richly appointed study, where they were greeted by the Manor's owner, Baron Giacomo Morbidini.

The Baron stood well over six feet tall, his shoulders impossibly broad, his thick gray hair cut severely short. At first glance, he seemed like a much younger man, certainly not out of his forties; but when he leaned forward into the light, two features gave away the Baron's true nature.

The first was his face, so worn and weathered that it seemed little more than a haggard mass of lines and wrinkles, a monument to extremely advanced age.

His eyes were the second. They glimmered from underneath shaggy gray brows, bright and clear and full of fierce intelligence—and red. Red as rubies. Red as blood.

When the Baron came out from behind his desk, he moved with the calm, powerful assurance of an athlete, but each movement was also accompanied by a sound. Hard to hear at first, but ultimately unmistakable: the whisper of metal gliding across oiled metal.

The Baron went to Sonnet first, bowed low, and kissed her hand as would a perfect gentleman. "You are beautiful as ever, Madam Ivandrova."

"As you are gracious, Baron," she answered.

He turned to Cromwell then and shook his hand, just firmly enough not to damage anything. The Baron *could* have closed his fingers around Cromwell's and squeezed until the smaller man's flesh and bone ground together into a mangled pulp. Cromwell knew that, but he simply looked the Baron in the eye and even smiled a little.

"What do you have for us, Giacomo?"

Sabre Cromwell was one of four people on the planet allowed to call Baron Morbidini by his first name.

The Baron turned back to his desk and motioned for Sonnet and Cromwell to come forward. "I have received some intelligence." His voice always emerged as a kind of contradiction—an inhuman basso growl couched in supremely proper inflections. His pronunciations were always crisp, even courtly. "More accurately, some intelligence we already possessed has been properly analyzed."

He gestured at the desktop where five glossy eight-by-ten photographs were displayed. "In the last two years, five of our operations have been either compromised or shut down entirely, almost certainly due to BGO involvement. Up until now, we had not been able to determine the identity of the primary operative involved. There seemed to be no common link between incidents."

Cromwell and Sonnet both peered at the photos. Sonnet's expression remained impassive, but Cromwell frowned. "What are we seeing here?"

The Baron sat down in a huge, steel-reinforced chair behind the desk, and steepled his fingers. "You are seeing the one person who has been observed in all five places at all five times. Dresden. Monaco. Warsaw. Johannesburg. And now Rio de Janeiro. We do not know her name yet. But I have decided that, whatever her identity, this young lady needs to be sanctioned."

Sonnet nodded, silent, thinking.

Cromwell's face slowly split into a predatory grin. "Where and how do we find her?"

The Baron's eyes glittered, revealing his ferocious, terrifying mind. "*That* is why I asked you here today."

From the desktop, five glossy photos of Alex Benno gazed up at them.

chapter five

Alex woke from a dream in which she was stuck in a cathedral's bell tower, the gonging of the bells rattling her brain. She realized it was someone ringing the doorbell. She shouted, "You don't have to *lean* on the button!" and got out of bed.

Pulling on a robe, Alex trudged over, peered through the peephole, and groaned. She threw back the locks and opened the door. Second-in-Command stood there looking impatient, her business attire impeccable.

Sec's version of hello was: "You don't answer your phone now?"

Alex turned and headed for the kitchen. "I didn't hear it." She glanced at a clock—8:42. She *had* been tired.

Sec followed her in. "Well, hurry up and get dressed, we've got a briefing in half an hour."

She watched as Alex dropped a filter pack into her single-cup coffeemaker.

"Since when do you drink coffee?"

Alex frowned. She wasn't sure if it was because of Sec's brusque demeanor or because she *just* got back from a mission or what, exactly, but she found herself feeling awfully intolerant. The truth was that the coffeemaker had come with the condo, kind of like Worsel the parrot, but instead of explaining that Alex said, "I *am* an adult now, you know."

Sec sighed. "Here we go with that again." Alex shot her a sharp look, but Sec went on. "You made enough noise about getting your own place, Alex, and wouldn't let *any* of us forget about your turning eighteen. Well, I know you know this already, but I'm going to say it again. Adults have responsibilities. Adults get up and go to work *every day*. Adults have obligations that they have to meet, no matter what."

Alex turned to face her. "Why are you lecturing me?"

Sec's visible impatience grew. "Because an adult wouldn't oversleep like a high-schooler on summer vacation. An adult would answer the phone when it rings."

Alex drew in a sharp breath. Words—a *lot* of words—flew into her mind. Words about obligations and responsibilities and how *laughable* it was for Sec to bring such things up to her. She felt her cheeks getting hot, and she clenched her teeth. She could see that Sec was just standing there waiting to hear it.

But after a few moments, Alex exhaled slowly, picked up her coffee cup and turned to leave the kitchen. "Give me a couple of minutes."

Sec folded her arms across her chest. "I'll be right here."

* * *

Alex rode with Sec in a Bureau car back to the Square.

As usual, the driver pretended he was alone in the car while Sec and Alex sat together in the back seat. After a couple of minutes in stop-and-go traffic, Sec's expression began to lighten, and she made an attempt at small talk.

"That last Prime was pretty impressive, wasn't she?"

Alex turned her face to the window so Sec couldn't see the eye-rolling. "Well, y'know. They *all* are."

"It never fails to amaze me. The specialization, I mean. I know we asked for the ultimate hostage negotiator, but what she did? Knowing *exactly* what to say to Lindsay like that? It was quite a treat to listen to."

Sec continued chattering about how spectacular Claudia had been until they arrived.

Alex tuned her out completely.

She'd been through all the security measures at the Square so often that, even though there were a lot of them, she did it more or less unconsciously—a rote set of movements, like brushing your teeth. She and Sec made their way toward the center of the building, heading for the briefing room and the preliminary meeting. They passed the door leading to the BGO dormitories, and Alex gave it a long, somewhat wistful glance. She knew Gail and Chuck were in there, right now, in class, and wished she could sneak back in and surprise them as they arrived at study hall. Instead, she followed Sec.

"Where's B.C.?" Alex asked.

"He's on his way. He said we could get started without him."

Alex *hmphed*.

The briefing room wasn't much to look at: spacious, oblong, with comfortable office chairs around a big circular table. In the table's center was a tiny lens; it was dark for now, inactive.

Sec closed the door. "All right, Alex, it's pretty straightforward this time. Have you ever heard of Vosarak?"

Alex sat down. In keeping with the rather uncharacteristic sullen rebellion she'd begun since she woke up, she propped her feet up on an adjacent chair. "No. What's Vosarak?"

Sec paused for a moment, frowning a little at Alex's feet, but went on. "Vosarak is an ancient, dead language. Nobody uses it anymore, and there are precious few examples of it in writing. No one is even sure where it originated, since two carvings were found in the Brazilian interior, and another was discovered buried in a temple in China."

Alex absently twirled one long strand of hair, not looking at Sec. "Okay."

Sec either didn't notice the bored tone in Alex's voice or chose not to acknowledge it. "What's even more mysterious is that, similar to Basque, Vosarak shares no known link to any other language on the planet. It seems to have simply appeared out of nowhere, fully evolved, with no connection to any people or culture."

"Right, okay," Alex said, finally turning to look at Sec. "What's all this got to do with me, then?"

Sec frowned more deeply and folded her arms across her chest again. "Alex, this is an *assignment* we're talking about here, not some list of chores. I would think you might take it a bit more seriously."

Alex stared at her. Her cheeks grew hot again, and she knew they must be practically glowing red. She slowly pushed the other chair away with her feet and stood up.

"You don't think I'm taking this *seriously?*"

Sec recoiled somewhat from Alex's tone, not so much out of fear as simple surprise. "I should have said this to you yesterday in the hallway, Alex, but I'll say it now. Please lower your voice."

"I don't feel like lowering my voice!" Alex said, even more loudly. "And I *really* don't feel like listening to *you* anymore! The Bureau's got *tons* of people on payroll who're older, smarter, better educated, and a hell of a lot more qualified than I am. Get one of *them* to handle this *assignment*. I'm leaving."

With Sec standing there, genuinely shocked now, Alex turned on her heel, marched to the briefing room's nearest door, yanked it open . . . and literally bounced off the chest of the man standing right outside.

B.C., the Bureau Chief, stood there for a moment, gazing down at Alex, his expression grim.

Alex stared right back up at him, unable to look away, feeling worse than the proverbial deer in headlights. Her anger evaporated instantly, along with any resolve she might have had, and she thought for a second that either her knees or her bladder might give way. Obviously, B.C. heard every word of her outburst.

Before Alex could speak, he said, "Come with me," then turned and walked away. Alex shot a glance back at Second-in-Command—who, if Alex read her expression correctly, was feeling pretty smug at this point—then followed after B.C. like a dog follows its master for a beating.

chapter six

The style and decor of the Bureau Chief's office reflected what Alex knew of his personality. She'd seen the room several times over the years, usually under much better circumstances, and it had never changed. The carpet, the oil portraits of people she'd never heard of on the walls, the chairs, even the items on his desk (right down to the No. 2 pencils, the lengths of which never changed), all of it remained perfectly ordered and perfectly consistent.

B.C. sat down behind his desk and waved Alex to one of the two chairs in front of it. She sat on the edge of her seat, looking down at the floor, her heart fluttering like a hummingbird in her chest.

"What was that back there?" B.C. asked conversationally. Alex glanced up, hoping that maybe he wasn't mad, but saw the little line that appeared between his eyebrows when he *was* mad. She stared at the floor again.

"It was—uh, nothing. Nothing, sir."

B.C. picked up a pencil with one hand and tapped the desk with it. Looking at just a photograph of the Bureau Chief, Alex knew, he wouldn't necessarily seem threatening: Middle-aged, always in a perfectly tailored suit, conservatively cut red hair that had faded mostly to white . . . he could have been a high school math teacher.

But in person, it was obvious why he was put in charge of one of the United States' most highly classified, closely guarded agencies.

"It didn't sound like nothing," he said, still completely calm. "This isn't like you, Alex. You've always been the best of the team players. What's made you unhappy?"

Alex exhaled, long and slow, then forced herself to look up into B.C.'s clear blue eyes. The line between his brows was still there, but she thought it might be a bit less severe now.

"I don't know how to put it into words, sir."

He leaned forward. "Would you mind if I conjectured?"

"Uh . . . well, uh, no, I don't guess I'd . . . uh, mind, no."

B.C. dropped his gaze to the pencil again. "Things have changed, but you're feeling as if they've either changed too much or haven't changed enough."

Alex sat back in her chair, listening intently.

B.C. went on, "You wanted more autonomy. That's why, when you turned eighteen, we got you your own place, put you on salary, let you start paying your own bills and such. But . . . and again, I'm just conjecturing . . . you think we still watch you too much, treat you the same way we did before. Is that accurate, would you say?"

"Um. Well . . . yeah, I guess so."

"At the same time, you miss your friends. You've grown up in such an insular environment, you don't feel you can truly fit into the world outside the BGO, and you're lonely. Also accurate?"

She grimaced and nodded.

B.C. sighed. "Alex, understand, we have no protocol in place for how to deal with you. As you're already aware, you are unique. We can't look back on our decades of experience and know precisely how to make you most comfortable."

"I know, sir, and it's really not the changes that—" *Oops.* Alex caught herself, but when she looked up at B.C. again, she saw that he had heard her perfectly.

"It's not the changes that . . . what? That bother you? Then what *does* bother you, Alex?"

Oh, God. The one thought she should have kept to herself at this moment. The one thing that was going to convince B.C. that Alex Benno had the maturity of a Dachshund puppy and should never have been allowed out of the dorms.

"It's . . ."

"Come on. Out with it."

Maybe it'll feel good to get this off my chest, Alex thought, more than a little desperately. She plunged ahead.

"I'm tired of not getting any recognition, sir."

"Excuse me?"

"All the Alex Primes, sir! Sure, they're incredibly talented, and smart—I mean, that's the whole *point*, and

I *know* they're crucial to the missions you send them on, but . . ."

"But?"

"But it's *me!* I'm the one responsible for all this! None of it would be happening if *I* weren't able to bring them here!"

Alex stood and paced around behind the chair. "Like yesterday. Okay? Right, Claudia went in and rescued the hostage and got the guy to give up the arms shipment. And I *know* how important that was, I *know* SKAR could've gotten their hands on it. But we get back, and today it's like—God, nobody even knew I was *there* at the party. I'm just, it's like, it's like everybody takes me so *completely* for granted, and . . ." Her words trailed off, and her knuckles had turned white as she gripped the back of the chair.

A thoughtful frown appeared on B.C.'s face. Alex was relieved to see that this was visibly different from the tiny line of anger he'd had before, especially since she was in totally uncharted waters.

She went on, "I know the Bureau's tried to do some nice stuff for me, now that I'm legal, but let's face it: if I decided to just walk away, say 'I quit,' just disappear and go have a normal life . . . would you let that happen? Be honest."

Very quietly, but without any hesitation, B.C. said, "No. No, you know we couldn't let that happen."

"Right. And you know what? I've accepted that. I've accepted that this is my life. But something's got to change, and change fast. Do you know what it's like seeing someone so perfect, so much *better* than I am, getting credit for all these missions that she couldn't even *be* on if it weren't for me? She's off doing all these . . . these *glorious* things, and you know where I am, every single time? I'm in the back of the van, half a mile away, bored out of my mind.

"It's the chaperones that drive me the craziest. These guys that make the chess club look like extreme sports, and I know they're there for my protection, but it's like I'm a prisoner! This apartment I've got now, the car, you know what Sec said when she gave me the keys to the car? She said, 'Okay, have fun, be sure not to leave the city.' "

One corner of B.C.'s mouth twitched upward. Alex didn't know how to interpret that, but she drew in a breath to keep talking—and realized she had nothing else to say.

B.C., still very quietly, asked, "Is there more?"

Alex shook her head. "I think I've lost my train of thought. I'm afraid if I go on now I'll either repeat myself or accidentally insult you."

He sighed, stood, and came around to the front of the desk, then leaned back on it and shoved his hands into his pockets. "Tell you what. This next assignment doesn't look like a hazardous one. If not for the language requirement, we *could* probably handle it with conventional means, as you so eloquently suggested to Second-in-Command."

Alex blushed.

B.C. went on. "You're right. You are eighteen; you are an adult. Let's try this one without the chaperones."

She blinked. "Are you serious?"

"I would ask you to use common sense, of course. But the danger factor on this mission should be nonexistent if our intelligence is correct."

"So . . ." She was still uncertain B.C. meant what she thought he meant. "So I can go on the next job . . . and I don't have to stay in the van?"

"You're an intelligent young woman who, I trust, will not put herself at any unnecessary risk." He paused, and the corner of his mouth twitched upward again. "Let's go get things started . . . and then perhaps you and Sec can discuss what's appropriate to wear in Paris this time of year."

Alex started for the door, feeling as if she were floating through some kind of waking dream.

Paris?

B.C. didn't follow her. "Go on back to the briefing room. I'll join you and Second-in-Command momentarily."

Alex couldn't speak; she just nodded mutely and left, a stunned expression on her face.

* * *

The Bureau Chief sat alone at his desk for several moments, eyes vacant, staring into space, his shoulders tense. Then he slumped, leaned forward and buried his face in his hands.

Without moving from that position, he said, "Gordon."

An intercom on his desk sprang to life, and a man's voice asked, "Sir?"

"Get me a list of our assets in Paris. Find out who's available for a discreet surveillance job."

"Right away, sir." The intercom clicked off again.

B.C. sighed, then pulled open his middle desk drawer and took out a manila folder. Inside the folder, on top of an inch-thick stack of files, was a black-and-white glossy photograph of a man and a woman. A casual observer, even at a glance, would have recognized them as Alex Benno's parents. The picture had been taken at a Bureau banquet; Mr. and Mrs. Benno stood, smiling, in front of a huge American flag hung on a wall.

"She's not ready yet," B.C. muttered to himself. "She's just not ready to know."

He closed the folder and put it back in his desk, then stood, straightened his jacket, and left the office.

chapter seven

Alex actually waited outside the briefing room for B.C. to join her before she went back in to talk to Sec. "Something wrong?" he asked, reaching past her for the door handle.

"Strength in numbers," she replied, a little sheepishly. She thought he might have found that amusing, but it was hard to tell.

Sec was waiting for them right where they had left her. "Everything worked out?" she asked primly.

"Everything is fine," B.C. answered, his tone completely neutral. Alex took that as a good sign and didn't say a word. "Now," he continued, "I believe Alex has the necessary information for the next step?"

Alex nodded. "Yep. Vosarak. Got it."

"Very good." B.C. headed for another door. Alex and Sec followed quietly, neither of them looking at the other just yet.

Alex knew the room they walked into better than she knew the bedroom in her new condo. Huge—not quite the size of an airplane hangar, but still awfully big—square, and bare, just featureless metal walls, ceiling, and floor. The gunmetal monotony was only broken in two places, first by the door they came in through, and second by an observation window and door on one side. Sec and B.C. both exited through that door, while Alex walked out to the middle of the floor and waited.

Sec's voice soon came over an unseen loudspeaker. "All right, Alex. We're ready when you are."

This was it. Showtime.

Alex bowed her head, closed her eyes, and said, "Right. Just . . . give me a minute . . . and . . ."

Her voice dissipated in mid-sentence, the words fading with a strange little echo. Ten seconds passed as she breathed steadily in and out.

And then her next exhalation emerged as a long white plume of vapor.

Here and there around the chamber, tiny ice crystals began to form in intricate patterns on the walls and floor.

"Come on," Alex whispered, calm, her breath visible as tiny puffs in the suddenly frigid air. "I know you're out there."

In the adjacent observation room, Sec sat at a bank of monitoring and analysis equipment. She grinned broadly, her irritation with Alex forgotten; B.C. stood behind her, emotionlesss, watching Alex through the one-way glass.

"This still gives me chills, you know," Sec said. "Even from over here."

"How are her vitals?"

Sec's eyes scanned across the instruments. "Normal. Like always."

B.C. said, "That's 'as' always."

In the main chamber, Alex's concentration deepened, and the air temperature dropped several more degrees. Then—slowly at first, very slowly—*snowflakes* began to fall from the ceiling.

Their number and frequency escalated rapidly, until Alex stood rooted to the spot in the middle of a full-blown snowfall.

Except that the snowflakes weren't *truly* snowflakes. Magnified high-speed film frames of this phenomenon revealed an astounding sight: at the center of each crystalline structure was, quite literally, a window to another world. And visible through those windows, in each and every snowflake, was a young woman.

The women varied just as much as the snowflakes themselves, in that no two were alike. But they also had one thing in common: in one way or another, ranging from shared facial features to eye color to hair texture or even the scattering of freckles across their noses, each of these women resembled Alex Benno.

Because each of them *was* Alex Benno.

That was the reason Alex had been raised in such an insulated, sheltered environment. That was the reason the Bureau wanted to keep her so safe. Alex Benno could look into an infinite number of alternate realities and see the version of herself that lived there. She could see them . . . and she could bring them to her reality.

A brief but powerful telepathic bond stretched out from Alex to every one of the snowflakes tumbling toward the cold, metal floor. She knew what to look for: an expert in the ancient, dead language called Vosarak. And she knew there must be one of her other selves that would qualify. The different dimensions stretched out into infinity; there *had* to be someone.

Her mind touched alternate after alternate. "Not you," she whispered. "Not you, either . . . come on . . . come on, let me see you . . ."

And then moments later she said, "Ah *ha.*"

One snowflake drifted lazily down to the floor about ten feet in front of her, while all the others faded and disappeared as if they had never been there at all.

Alex kept her eyes focused on the remaining snowflake as it touched down. She didn't even blink as a column of golden light sprang up from the floor where the flake landed.

The light flared, blinding, bright as the sun. When it faded, the latest Alex Prime stood there amid the dwindling crackles and sparks of energy that always accompanied an Invitation.

Alex looked her over.

Tall, as usual. Alex had yet to summon an alternate shorter than she was, but since she charted at barely five foot one, that wasn't saying much. Gorgeous, as usual, too; this one looked as if she'd been raised on the beach. Her sandals, shorts, and tanktop showed off her long, tanned, muscular limbs to great effect. She had a head of dark curls, just as Alex did, but hers looked very soft. Alex had never been able to make her own hair feel like anything but wire. Plus, the alternate's had a lot of blonde highlights, no doubt from countless hours spent in the sun.

Alex had never been to the ocean.

After a few moments, the alternate turned to Alex, grinned broadly, and extended a good-natured hand. "Hi!" Her voice practically bubbled with positive energy. "It's *great* to meet you. I'm Alex Benno."

"Yeah, yeah," Alex said, shaking the offered hand. "I know. So am I."

chapter eight

Ten minutes later, Alex and the newest Code-Name Alex Prime stood in a room on the Square's top floor, looking through a huge plateglass window at the city that stretched out before them.

"Wow." The taller of the two touched the glass lightly. "It's . . . well, it's a whole lot like the Washington, D.C. I'm familiar with."

"Yeah," Alex said. "The differences are usually pretty subtle, but they're there. Listen, if we both use the same name, things'll get tangled up pretty fast. What we usually do is call you by your middle name to keep it straight."

"Rachel?" She considered it for a moment. "Sure, I guess that'd be okay. I've never gone by my middle name before."

Alex went on, covering the usual material. "Okay, so I know you're willing to help—you made that clear when I contacted you telepathically. But now that you're here, do you have any questions?"

Rachel thought for a moment, twirling one curl of silky hair around a finger as she did. "Questions . . . hmm . . ."

Alex waited. She figured Rachel would come up with some sort of clever or profound pronouncement, since the Alex Primes *usually* did at this point. She was totally caught off guard when Rachel said, "I—it's just—sorry, this is just so *cool!*"

"Excuse me?"

Rachel seemed to be serious. "I mean, God, do you know how unlikely it is that *I'd* be asked for help . . . ? Not just because I know this language that hardly anybody's ever heard of . . . but never mind that, I'm in a whole other freaking *world!* Is there—" She seemed to gather her thoughts, recouping a little of her expected poise. "Um. When do I get all the details?"

"We're about to have a briefing," Alex answered, not sure what to make of her counterpart. "Sec . . . that's Second-in-Command . . . and the Bureau Chief will fill us in."

"Okay." Rachel hesitated. "Do these people have real names?"

"You don't get to know them. *I* don't even know them. But it's okay; they're all right. Well, B.C. is, anyway. C'mon, I'll take you down to the briefing room."

Alex led Rachel onto another elevator and hit the appropriate button. Beside her, Rachel giggled; Alex shot her a quizzical look.

"Sorry," Rachel said. "I pretty much know the hows and whys—that all came through when you contacted me. It's just a lot to take in. And not just for me, I mean, my God, I can't even imagine what this must be like for *you!* It's just a one-time deal for me, right? But you go through this all the time. How do you stay sane?"

Alex was so immeasurably surprised by this question that for a moment she forgot to breathe. None of the Alex Primes had ever asked her that before. *Ever.* She didn't know what to say.

"You, uh . . . you want to talk about . . . me?"

"Well *yeah.* Why wouldn't I?"

But then the elevator doors opened, and Sec was waiting for them. "Right this way, please," she said, and Alex followed mutely, Rachel behind her.

In the briefing room, Sec and B.C. both stood, while Alex and Rachel took seats at the table. Sec did almost all the talking, while B.C. simply hovered near the door and observed.

Sec said, "Projector," and the room's lights dimmed. Then the lens set in the center of the table flickered and shot a cone of light at the ceiling; immediately the cone narrowed and became a three-dimensional holographic image of a sword suspended vertically in the air. It looked very old. It also looked brutal and deadly, with a long, broad, heavy blade—the kind meant to break and crush as well as cut.

"This is your objective," Sec said.

Alex and Rachel both leaned forward to look at it. Alex squinted; there was something on the blade, but she couldn't tell exactly what it was.

Rachel didn't have that problem. "Oh my *God*," she said, her voice quivering with excitement.

Thinking she was missing something obvious, Alex stood up and leaned farther forward. Now she saw that the sword's blade had two different kinds of writing etched into it. She still didn't recognize either one, and was about to glance over at Rachel to see if they had any meaning for her, when Rachel almost knocked her down scrambling forward to stare at the sword.

"Sorry, sorry," Rachel mumbled, reaching out to steady Alex with a hand on her shoulder, but her eyes never left the holographic display. "That's Vosarak," she breathed, "and . . . Aramaic!"

"Correct," Sec stated. "The sword was discovered in a temple in China six months ago."

Rachel sat back down. Alex saw her do it out of the corner of her eye and sat down, too.

Sec went on. "I'm sure I don't have to tell *you* how significant this is. It's easily as important as the discovery of the Rosetta Stone. For the first time, linguistic anthropologists have a chance at accurately translating Vosarak."

Rachel seemed on the verge of tears. More out of curiosity than concern, Alex asked, "Are you okay?"

Rachel blinked a few times. "Yeah. Yes. I'm *better* than okay. It's just—this is something I've studied, something I've worked on my whole life. But all I've had so far are *theories*, and now this. I'm, ah, I'm a little excited, that's all." She seemed a good bit more than just a *little* excited.

"Which is why you're here." Sec clearly wanted to get on with things. "The long and the short of it is this: before any truly in-depth analysis could be made of what's being called the Vosarak Sword, the artifact was stolen."

Rachel gasped, small and sharp, as if she'd suffered a sudden stabbing pain.

"Now, in the grand scheme of things, we had more and bigger issues to worry about than the theft of one obscure archaeological exhibit. Until three weeks ago, when our computer security division became aware of a new virus trying to propagate through the Internet.

"It seemed to be little more than a test run. But the disturbing factor here is that one line of the computer code contained a word in Vosarak."

Alex watched Rachel's reaction. Her brows began to knit, slowly drawing together. "Go on," Rachel said.

"The virus containing the word in question is designed to hack secure financial records. We suspect that if left unchecked, this virus could ultimately compromise every major financial institution on the planet."

Rachel sat back in her chair. "Who's behind this? Do you know?"

Out of the corner of her eye, Alex saw B.C. shift position, his body language tensing up. Sec continued, "We don't have proof, but we have very strong suspicions."

The holographic sword blurred and resolved into the image of a tall, powerfully built elderly man with a shock of gray hair and grotesquely luminous red eyes. The image moved like a 3-D film clip. The man, dressed in a heavy overcoat, strolled down a sidewalk beside a road dotted with patches of snow.

After a few seconds, the image reset and began to play over, on a loop.

"This is Baron Giacomo Morbidini, known in some circles as the Gray Baron. Morbidini claims to be the illegitimate son of Benito Mussolini, the fascist dictator of Italy during World War II."

Rachel seemed darkly fascinated. "I know who Benito Mussolini was."

"Details change," Alex said. "Our history doesn't always follow your history."

Rachel nodded as if to say *all right*. "Why are his eyes red?"

Sec answered. "We can't say for sure, but the rumor is that Morbidini is more machine than human. That would certainly go a long way toward explaining his apparent health at such an old age."

Alex smiled. "Yeah, sometimes we call him Darth Vaderini."

Polite but clearly confused, Rachel said, "Excuse me?"

Alex raised her eyebrows. She could tell Rachel had no idea what she was talking about. *Guess George Lucas screwed up somewhere in Rachel's world.* "Never mind. Not important."

Sec scowled, irritated at the interruption. "Morbidini is one of three founders of an organization called SKAR—the Sacred Knights of Altered Reality. Consisting of members of various fanatical religious and political splinter sects, SKAR's stated goal is to 'bring the Earth to a state of perfect peace and harmony.'"

"Let me guess," Rachel said. "It's *their* definition of perfect peace and harmony, and they've decided to achieve it by whatever means *they* deem necessary."

Alex said, "Pretty much." She kept watching Rachel. "SKAR's got some crazy high-tech weapons and gizmos, and the Gray Baron looks like the one responsible for it all."

"Hmm. Okay. You said he was one of three founders. Who are the other two?"

"Real winners," Sec replied with a pointed look at Alex that meant *this is my briefing.* "There's this chap . . ." The hologram blurred again, then shifted to an image of a tall, expensively dressed, rail-thin man walking out of what looked like a five-star hotel. He would have had movie-star good looks if his face weren't so menacing. His cruelty was obvious.

"Sabre Cromwell. Raised by a group of Freemason extremists. Quite possibly the deadliest hand-to-hand combatant on the face of the earth, and every bit as dedicated as the Baron to transforming Earth into the SKAR Happy Fun Park.

"And the third." As the lens flickered again, Alex snuck a quick look at Sec. A couple of times before, she'd heard a note of serious bitterness in Sec's voice when discussing this particular person. Alex had tried to find the right time to ask Sec about it, but the right time had yet to arise.

Sabre Cromwell's holographic film clip gave way to that of a breathtakingly beautiful woman. Long, jet-black hair; alabaster skin that had never known even a hint of blemish; startling, ice-blue eyes . . . She wore a low-cut, not-quite-scandalous evening gown, held a martini glass, and laughed at a joke made by someone unseen.

"Sonnet Ivandrova." Sec's voice came out brittle as she said the name. "Born in Russia but raised primarily in London. Her parents belonged to an insane, ultra-secret cult that worshiped the ghost of Rasputin, the mad Russian monk. She's loyal to SKAR, but seems even more interested in the day when her parents' brand of black magic can be turned loose on the world."

Alex was pretty sure Rachel had also picked up on Sec's emotional reaction to Sonnet Ivandrova. But Rachel didn't mention it; what she said—with a respectful amount of skepticism—was, "Magic?"

All three heads turned as B.C. spoke up for the first time. "We don't know that it is magic," he said calmly. "The rumors of that are even flimsier than the ones concerning Baron Morbidini's body parts. But we have had reports from field agents, more than once, claiming that Sonnet Ivandrova can do things unexplained by current science. These reports have come from men and women whose word is beyond reproach."

That was all he'd wanted to say. Folding his arms, he leaned back against the wall again.

"Well." Rachel just took it all in. "Magic. Hm."

Sec said, "SKAR does not have an official militia; on rare occasions we've documented them hiring mercenaries for overtly militaristic actions. But what it *does* have is a vast network of operatives across the globe, nearly all of whom are sleeper agents. A SKAR operative can be anywhere, at any time, and when activated will behave with utmost loyalty to his or her cause."

"Huh." Rachel frowned, thinking. "Is there a method for spotting one?"

"No, unfortunately," Sec said. "An operative might be anybody from a cop to a housewife."

"Grand," Rachel breathed out. "So what you're telling me is that a group of dangerous weirdo fanatics want to take over the world—"

"Nah, not take it over," Alex interjected. "Just *fix* it."

Rachel took that in stride. "That's just as bad. So they want to fix the world, and this computer virus might give them the boost they need to do it."

"That's correct," Sec answered. "We're already mobilized in an effort to track the sword down, but you are uniquely qualified to understand it and things related to it, since you know more about Vosarak than literally anyone else on the planet. We need you to talk to people and help us find the sword, so we can either get it back or get a detailed analysis of it."

Rachel took a few moments, considering. Then she grinned again. "Sounds like fun. Where do I start, and when do I leave?"

Alex closed her eyes at the word "I."

B.C. spoke again. "It's not just you. While you are here, you can be separated from Alex by no more than half a mile.

Otherwise you will return immediately to your world, and I'm afraid it's a one-way trip. Therefore, Alex will accompany you on this assignment."

Rachel looked over at Alex. She didn't seem to mind the idea. "Yeah, okay. Well, then. When do *we* leave?"

Alex couldn't help herself. "You don't care that I have to go with you?"

"Why should I object? You're legal, right? We'll have fun."

B.C. said, "Good. Let's get you both down to tech support for your sensors."

As they left the room, Rachel murmured to Alex, "What sensors?" But Alex was still too stunned by Rachel's attitude to answer.

chapter nine

Beneath Baron Morbidini's ancestral mansion, the classic and opulent surroundings gave way to a modern and advanced decor. Decades earlier, the Baron had overseen the construction of a massive state-of-the-art laboratory underneath his home, and had made certain that with each year the lab would boast the latest scientific advances the world had to offer.

This was not born out of scientific curiosity. It was self-preservation.

Forty-seven scientists lived and worked in this lab complex. Most of them specialized either in researching new power sources or developing new weapons; but between twelve and fifteen of them, depending on the need, devoted one hundred percent of their time to maintaining the Baron's body. His staggering biomechanical necessities increased in severity with each passing year.

A lot can be accomplished with the proper budget, though . . . and to say the Baron's wealth was vast would be a sharp understatement.

An hour after Sabre Cromwell and Sonnet Ivandrova had left, Doctor Doug Slotnick and Doctor Ami Grossman sat down at a workbench in one of the complex's labs. They'd worked for the Baron for three and four years, respectively. Never in all that time had they been as terrified as they were now.

Slotnick was in the process of turning a pale shade of green.

Grossman couldn't stop riffling through a sheaf of papers, mumbling, "It's in here, it's got to be, it's in here, I know it is."

His voice weak, Slotnick said, "What do we *do*? How do we tell the Baron about this?"

Grossman ignored him. "It's in here. I know it is. It's got to be."

Slotnick got up from his stool and snatched the papers away from Grossman, who blinked at him with glazed eyes.

Grossman said, "Maybe, uh, m-maybe he won't check on things until we figure this out?"

Slotnick was about to start yelling at his colleague when they both froze in place.

The Baron was coming.

They could hear his footsteps. More important, they could *feel* his footsteps, as tiny impact tremors vibrated through the floor beneath them. It reminded them of his true nature.

The nearest wall's door slid open and the Baron entered, ducking his head slightly. He paused to study the two scientists, and then his craggy, weathered face clenched into a scowl.

"What has happened?"

Slotnick and Grossman traded glances. Then Grossman stood, took the sheaf of papers from Slotnick, and handed them mutely to the Baron. "We only just discovered this, sir."

Morbidini took the papers, still scowling, and scanned over the data presented there; he read with inhuman speed, thumbing through the pages like someone looking something up in a phone book. When he had finished, his scowl grew even darker—something the two scientists hadn't thought possible.

"*Why* is this happening?" the Baron growled.

Slotnick cleared his throat. "Well, sir, it's . . . it's actually to be expected when running a system this complex, involving this many unknown factors; the law of averages *alone* would dictate that entropy would present itself in—"

The Baron took a thunderous step forward and slammed one hand down on a heavy steel countertop. The metal crumpled around his knuckles as if it were aluminum foil.

"This effect is happening at *random?*"

"It's because of the tests involving radio," Grossman said meekly. "The signal should have been completely hidden, but some part of it seems to have . . . uh . . . leaked out."

Morbidini drew very close to Grossman, so close that the red of the Baron's eyes reflected clearly in Grossman's own. Standing nearby, Slotnick fought hard to control his bowels.

"Fix this," the Baron hissed. "I cannot think of many things more conspicuous than subjects with incomplete programming activating spontaneously across the globe.

We do not *need* drooling idiots stumbling about, trying to fulfill half-understood SKAR agendas." He glared at them for a few seconds. "If you are *unable* to fix this . . ." His luminous crimson eyes darted meaningfully at the mangled countertop.

The Baron then turned and left the room.

Grossman started crying.

Slotnick, mildly proud of himself that he hadn't soiled his pants, said, "Come on. Knock that off. We've got a lot of work to do."

chapter ten

Tech support was two floors down, so it didn't take long to get there. Alex and Rachel were both given what at first glance looked like stylish wristwatches. The tech on duty, a stern woman named Plimpton, explained their function in a weary, monotone voice.

"Your time here," she droned, addressing Rachel, "is dependent on your proximity to young Alex. These sensors are keyed to each other. When you press this button, an LED pointer will appear, designed to look like a second hand, indicating the location of the other sensor. Additionally, the window that usually displays the date will flash the distance in feet, yards, or meters, your choice. *Do not* get more than half a mile away from each other. If you're in danger of exceeding the distance limit, the watch face will glow red. Understand?"

"Yes, ma'am," Rachel said.

"Good. You should get to wardrobe."

Walking out into the hallway, Rachel repeated, "Wardrobe?"

Alex realized Rachel was waiting for a response from her. "Well—you've got to have more than one pair of clothes to wear, right?"

Rachel gave a small shrug. "I *was* wondering about that, yeah."

"So, come with me." Alex led the way around a corner and opened an unmarked door. "They're pretty well stocked."

Alex led Rachel into a room that looked like a small warehouse. Shelf after shelf and rack after rack of tightly packed clothing filled the space, as if a three-floor department store had been jammed into a five-car garage. There was also a collection of fashion magazines on a table beside a small bench.

Rachel took a couple of steps in and peered around with wide eyes. "It, uh . . . There . . . seems to be quite the variety."

"Yeah." Alex let the door close behind her, then leaned against it. She planned to excuse herself in a couple of seconds, since this part of the process was excruciatingly boring for her. "There ought to be a few different styles you'll find appealing, and the sizes should be right. There's sort of a predictable range with that."

Rachel turned around to face her, one eyebrow cocked up. "Hang on. Are you saying all this"—she waved one arm around—"is for me? Just *me?*"

Alex nodded. "I'll leave you to it, okay?"

She turned to go, but Rachel stepped forward quickly. "Wait, wait a minute . . . ! How much do I take? Do I get luggage?"

"Um. Usually a week's worth is good, maybe two. They'll give you luggage according to how much stuff you pick."

Rachel glanced around again, starting to smile now, then lifted both arms and pivoted in place. "So . . . basically . . . I get to go shopping. And it's all free."

"Yeah, I guess you could think of it like that."

Alex couldn't help but grin a little. It had been a while since she'd summoned an Alex Prime this playful; more often than not they were either completely all-business-no-fun, or totally wrapped up in themselves. Like that last one . . .

Rachel's eyes twinkled. "Well, c'mon, you can't just leave! I hate shopping alone. You have to help me pick out what I'm going to wear."

Okay, this is too weird. None of the alternates *ever* treated Alex as an equal.

"I don't know that I'd be much help. I've, uh . . . I haven't done much shopping myself before, and . . . I don't have much fashion sense."

Rachel eyed Alex's sneakers, jeans, and baggy sweater. "There's nothing wrong with what you're wearing now. C'mon, please?"

Please? Incredible.

"Yeah . . . yeah, okay. Here, they usually have a cart or something around to pile stuff on . . ."

Slightly less than an hour later, Rachel had picked out six different outfits. Alex didn't know if she'd actually helped in the selection process, but Rachel kept asking for her opinion, so she gave it. Along the way they chatted about things, like what kind of makeup would best complement Alex's hair color, or the various clothing styles Rachel liked from one of the copies of *COSMOgirl!*

Tentatively, Alex sat down on the bench and flipped through a magazine. She wasn't really interested in the pictures of clothes or the quizzes, but an article titled "Be Your Own Hero" caught her eye. There was a list of celebrities with heroic qualities that girls could choose as their role models—some sort of confidence booster exercise. Alex's eye skimmed the article and then strayed back to the title "Be Your Own Hero."

Easier said than done for some people. She thought about all those times she'd had to sit in the van while her alternate version got to go on amazing adventures . . . *I'm always stuck as my own sidekick.*

"Alex?"

She snapped out of it at the sound of Rachel's voice. "Huh?"

"I said, so tell me about yourself," Rachel repeated, critically examining a pair of corduroy pants. "You must have a life like the female James Bond, huh? Or doesn't that character exist here?"

Alex stopped herself from snorting, and put down the magazine. "Yeah, we've got James Bond, but I'm nothing like that at all. I—there's, well, there's really not much to tell, honestly." Striving for a subject change, she said, "How about you? What do you do for a living? Must be something with language. Are you a professor?"

Rachel laughed. And there it was: that same *perfect*, chiming laugh that every Alex Prime had. It was a laugh that Alex had come to loathe, and she all but gritted her teeth at the sound of it.

"Nah, actually, the whole language thing is a hobby. I'm a firefighter."

That stopped Alex cold. A *firefighter?*

"You don't make a living with your language skills? But . . . you're better with languages than anybody else. Like, *anybody* else. How many do you speak?"

"Twenty-seven, fluently. I know dirty words in a couple dozen more."

"Then why not *use* that?" Alex still felt uncomfortable with the whole hanging-out-and-talking experience, and she hadn't intended to ask Rachel so much, but this was just flabbergasting.

Rachel shrugged. "It's something I like to do in my spare time. My job with the fire department's a lot more tangible. Y'know? The kind of thing I can really see, like, right away."

Alex hesitated. "Sort of, uh, an instant gratification thing?"

"Sometimes it's instant, yeah. It's never *delayed* gratification, in any case."

While Alex thought that over, she followed Rachel to another set of shelves, then watched as Rachel picked up a lacy black-and-pink thong. Mischievously, Rachel said, "I guess the Bureau wants me prepared for *any* eventuality, huh?"

Alex looked away, blushing. Rachel either didn't notice her embarrassment or pretended not to. Instead she picked up the matching bra. "Too bad I won't be able to take any of this stuff back with me once all this is over. Donal would love this set."

Carefully neutral, Alex asked, "Is Donal your boyfriend?"

Rachel nodded. "Boyfriend now. With any luck, fiancé sometime soon. If he ever gets over his jitters." She didn't really seem all that concerned about Donal's jitters. "How about you? You got somebody who'd appreciate something like this?"

Alex's eyes got huge. She sputtered for a few seconds, during which Rachel realized she'd crossed a line. "Oh, hey, I'm sorry, I'm sorry. I didn't mean to offend you."

Alex frowned. "It's not, it's . . . Y-you didn't offend me." Of *course* Rachel had offended her. "It's just really, uh . . . *personal*. I, ah, I don't—no, I don't have a boyfriend."

Rachel stayed silent for a few moments. Alex was sure Rachel could tell that she'd *never* had a boyfriend. Finally Rachel said, "Well, still. You should try some of these on."

"Excuse me? And the point of that would be *what?* Never mind that there's not a single bra here that would fit me."

Rachel rummaged through a few more thongs. "Bras, maybe not, but I think there's some panties here in your size."

Alex frowned, wavering between being further offended and just confused. "Okay, and I'll say it again, the point of that would be what? I already said I don't have a boyfriend."

Rachel turned and leaned against the shelf. She looked patient. "Wearing something beautiful and silky and lacy like this isn't just about showing it off, Alex. It's about having a secret."

Alex blinked. "Huh?"

"So you're walking down the street in your jeans and your baggy sweater, and that's all anybody sees on the outside, right? But if you're wearing these underneath . . ." She held up a pair of panties made of black lace decorated with small white silk hearts. "Then you know something nobody else knows. Something just for you. It can make you powerful. And *that* they *will* see."

Alex didn't know what to say.

"Anyway," Rachel turned and tossed the black-and-white panties back onto the shelf, "just something to think about." She went on with the selection.

Alex thought for a moment, quickly ripped out the article from COSMOgirl! and then silently trailed after Rachel.

chapter eleven

While Rachel and Alex were picking out clothes, a telephone rang in an opulent villa in the south of France. Sabre Cromwell motioned with his chin toward the phone, saying, "Whoever it is, tell them I'm busy." One of his servants scampered to pick up the receiver.

Cromwell stood in the center of the dojo he'd built as an addition to the house. He was indeed busy, as he currently faced twelve very large men, all of whom he had paid to try to beat the life out of him. Several of the men held weapons: nightsticks, knives—a couple of them even had guns.

Cromwell was unarmed and wore only a judo *gi.*

He started to motion the men forward, but the servant, a drab little man who excelled at laundering Cromwell's insanely expensive wardrobe, called out, "It's Mister Gray, sir. He says it's urgent."

Cromwell smiled. *Mister Gray.* That would be Baron Morbidini, of course. "In that case, ask him to hold on for maybe half a minute."

"Very good, sir."

While the servant relayed that message, Cromwell beckoned to the small crowd, who obligingly rushed forward. They knew better than to hold back, and so it was with great sincerity and enthusiasm that they attempted to bludgeon, stab, and shoot the man in front of them.

* * *

Sabre Cromwell was born Hershel Landon Spivak. His father abandoned the family when Hershel was barely a week old, leaving Greta, Hershel's uneducated mother, to do the best she could. Greta fared better than some women in her situation might have; she never started drinking or using drugs, never got involved in anything illegal. What she did do was work two and sometimes three menial, low-paying jobs at a time, leaving her son in the care of whatever neighbor or friend she could persuade to watch him.

It was a hard, joyless existence for the two of them, and it kept up that way until Hershel turned six.

A few days after her son's sixth birthday, Greta brought home a gentleman friend: a tall, severe man named Gustav Cromwell. Gustav immediately took a great interest in Hershel, and soon Gustav Cromwell married Greta and adopted him.

It wasn't until after the marriage that Gustav revealed several important facts. First: Hershel, not his mother, had first caught Gustav's attention. Gustav had seen Hershel on the street one day, fighting with two other boys, and immediately recognized within him a rare and powerful potential.

Second: Gustav was a member of a cultlike splinter sect of the Freemasons, the clandestine organization that some people believed secretly controlled the world. Gustav's group wanted to take that a step further and remove any doubt. World domination lay at the center of their beliefs.

Third: Gustav Cromwell intended to train, shape, and mold his adopted son into an unstoppable enforcer. Accordingly, he legally changed Hershel's name to Sabre, since the boy would become the sword that delivered the true peace and order Gustav craved. Leaving Greta no choice in the matter, Gustav relocated the family to Australia and began Sabre's training.

Gustav was not wrong about Sabre's potential. Hiring teacher after teacher, Gustav had the boy trained in virtually every known form of hand-to-hand (as well as armed) combat, and the boy thrived in his new environment. Wreaking destruction was second nature to him. Gustav let Sabre know that he'd never seen a student learn so quickly.

But it wasn't just physical training. Gustav Cromwell filled Sabre's mind with all of the philosophy and rhetoric of his splinter-sect ideals, quickly turning Sabre into the most zealous of followers.

The training continued until Sabre turned twenty-five, when Gustav was convinced that Sabre Cromwell had become the deadliest man on the planet. He then introduced Sabre to the one person who could best facilitate the splinter-sect's dreams coming true: Baron Giacomo Morbidini.

* * *

From the edge of the room, the servant winced as Cromwell sprang into a blur of action. His attackers seemed like dominoes, one falling down after the other; Cromwell moved wraithlike among them, spinning and weaving. His hands, elbows, knees, and feet all whipped out delivering splintering blows.

Maybe twenty seconds had passed before Cromwell was left facing one man: a huge, scarred mercenary named Galvez. And Galvez held a gun.

Cromwell was caught point-blank. Galvez had him completely at his mercy. No one, not Jackie Chan or Bruce Lee in their prime, *no one* could move faster than a bullet.

But Sabre Cromwell knew it wasn't a question of moving faster than a bullet. It was a question of moving faster than the trigger finger. Before Galvez could react, Cromwell sped forward and, grinning, slammed the heels of his hands together onto his opponent's wrist.

Galvez's fingers spasmed. Cromwell's strike had paralyzed the tendons in his hand. The gun dropped.

Still grinning, Cromwell wheeled around and kicked Galvez's temple. The man's unconscious body immediately hit the floor to join the other eleven passed-out fighters.

Exactly thirty seconds after he had last spoken to the servant, Cromwell walked over and picked up the phone.

"Paris is nice this time of year," the familiar, rumbling voice said.

"Oh, I couldn't agree more," Cromwell replied, and then hung up the phone without further ado. Turning to the servant, he said, "Have my charcoal Armani ready for me. I'm going to go take a shower, and then I'll be leaving."

"Very good, sir," the servant said. "Shall I ask these gentlemen to vacate the premises when they regain consciousness?"

"Whatever." Cromwell turned to leave the dojo. He had already forgotten about the fight.

As he walked, under his breath he sang the lyrics to an old rock song: "What's your name . . . little girl?"

chapter twelve

Boarding the transatlantic flight, Alex felt cautiously optimistic. On every other long flight, boat ride, or car trip—and there had been plenty of long ones—she had found herself bored stiff. She'd get motion sickness if she read, and she'd never found a video game that could hold her interest for any length of time.

But the current Alex Prime was like a revelation to her, despite a tendency to ask uncomfortable questions. Alex thought she'd finally figured out exactly what was happening: every other Prime had treated her like a child, because she'd *been* a child. Now she was an adult, and things were different.

Whatever the reason, she really hoped Rachel's friendliness would continue on the flight. Maybe these five hours wouldn't have to be unendurable.

* * *

Later, Alex would look back on that notion and think to herself, *I should've known better.*

They didn't travel by commercial airline; they couldn't exactly fly around the world using their own identities, since Alex needed to remain discreet and Rachel simply didn't have one. So they did the usual BGO dance: receiving IDs and papers from Sec on the way to the airport and flying on a private Bureau jet that masqueraded as a corporate plane.

That was another reason for the boredom, actually. If Alex had flown on a regular plane—*Seat 27A, window, no meal provided but we will be serving peanuts and coffee*—she could have done some people-watching. Or at least she was pretty sure she could have, judging by all the movies and TV shows she'd seen with planes in them.

Alex had never set foot on a commercial airplane before.

But there was definitely no people-watching on these assignment flights. Just her; the Alex Prime du jour; seven or eight huge, silent men in gray suits; and occasionally Sec.

Everything started out well enough. Better than usual, even. For one thing, the fleet of "mute-suits" was nowhere to be found, and for another, Rachel seemed just as eager to talk to Alex now as she had been when picking out her wardrobe. They chatted idly about music and their favorite movies.

But as soon as they got settled into their seats, Rachel reclined hers all the way back, tucked a pillow under her head and closed her eyes.

"Um . . . what're you doing?" Alex asked, then winced at how lame that came out.

Rachel took the lameness in stride; she opened one eye and good-naturedly said, "Is that a trick question?"

"I, uh . . . I just thought we could keep talking, is all."

Closing the eye again, Rachel said, "Give me half an hour, okay? I always sleep through takeoff. Makes the whole flight go a lot smoother for me."

Alex didn't like that, but she couldn't come up with any reason why it was unfair. She said, "Okay," and stared out the window until they were airborne.

Rachel looked incredibly peaceful, snoozing away in her seat. Alex thought back to part of their conversation earlier, when Rachel had told her about Donal, her maybe-fiancé back home. Donal turned out to be a super-smart, super-talented guy who designed ringtones for a cellphone company as his day job and played in a band on the weekends.

Alex wanted to continue talking about Donal, about men in general, really, and began to get more than a little impatient as Rachel kept on sleeping.

Finally, after they'd been in the air for (Alex checked) forty-two minutes, Rachel awoke with a start. She frowned, an expression Alex hadn't seen on her face yet, and quickly put her seat upright.

"How was your nap?" Alex asked, hopeful.

But something had changed. The easygoing demeanor had disappeared, replaced by tension. Rachel looked around, and then when she spoke to Alex it was hardly the conversation starter Alex had expected.

"Do you have anything to write on? A notebook, something like that?"

"Um . . . let me check." Alex rooted through the knapsack she usually carried instead of a purse. "Not, uh, not really anything to write *on*, but I've got something to write *with*." Grimacing at it, she held up a pink pen with a big ball of purple feathers on one end. "I mean, if you, uh . . . if you *want* to write with this thing."

Rachel accepted the pen with a mumbled "Thanks," then got up and went to the bathroom; she came back seconds later with a stack of folded paper towels, sat down and started writing something. Or possibly drawing; Alex couldn't see at that angle.

"Are you okay? Is something wrong?"

Rachel didn't look up at Alex when she answered. "I'm fine, I'm fine. I just . . ." She trailed off, still writing.

After several seconds of silence, Alex prompted, "You just . . . ?"

Rachel looked up, a bit sharply. "I'm sorry, Alex, could you just give me a little space here?" Then she went back to her paper towels without saying anything else.

Hurt, Alex stood, stepped past Rachel, and went to another row of seats at the opposite end of the cabin, where she sat down next to the window. Rachel didn't seem to notice.

The rest of the flight passed in stony silence.

* * *

Once they touched down at Charles de Gaulle, Alex managed to forget about Rachel's bizarre behavior for a while; on every other trip, the most she'd gotten to see of her surroundings at the airport was a few seconds of asphalt and sky (usually overcast; that was her luck) while being shuttled from the plane to the waiting armored van.

Today was different. Gloriously, fantastically different. B.C. really seemed to be keeping his word, allowing her to have the kind of autonomy that only Alex Prime had been given on these assignments in the past. Alex and Rachel exited the plane together, collected their luggage, and walked out into the terminal like . . . well, like *normal* people would.

Alex looked around eagerly as they left customs and made their way toward ground transportation (they'd be taking the train to travel the fourteen or so miles into Paris proper). She didn't know how the airport looked to people who were accustomed to seeing it, but to her it was a place of futuristic beauty, all curved walls and glass. An elderly lady passed by them, and Alex considered trying to say something in French. Maybe "Hello." or "Good day." She'd taken a year of French in school—she ought to remember that much.

Nothing came to her. Not a single word. And the more she tried to remember, the less she could find anything.

This didn't surprise her, after a couple seconds' thought. Several times in the past, on other missions, she'd experienced an odd sort of . . . disability, she guessed it could be called. Whatever Alex Prime specialized in, Alex herself lost. When her alternate was a theoretical physicist, all of Alex's basic math went out the window. When Alex Prime needed to be a brilliant dancer, Alex got clumsy. And since Rachel was a linguistic genius, Alex's language skills were suffering. It wouldn't have surprised her too much if she started forgetting how to speak English.

Rachel finally began to chat a little bit halfway through the train ride, but Alex could tell something was still bothering her. All her small talk and funny stories about Donal had dried up.

"Ever been to Paris before?" Rachel asked.

"Not like this." Alex tried to keep her voice pleasant. "I was here—well, *near* here, about three years ago. But it's not like I saw the city or anything."

Rachel thought about that. "I guess it makes sense, how they've been treating you."

"Oh." Great, now Rachel was spouting the company line. "You think so, huh?"

"Well, not that it was the right thing to do as far as *you're* concerned . . . and by you, I mean you as a person. Your happiness. But look at it from their perspective, and you're like the crown jewels, y'know? Someone as valuable as you are, of *course* they're going to want to keep you in a vault."

Alex chewed on her lower lip. *I'm like the crown jewels? Hmm.*

"Well, I'll tell you something," Alex said. "The view from the vault sucks."

Rachel laughed.

They chatted about inconsequential things for the rest of the train ride, and then hardly spoke at all in the taxi once they got into the city. But Alex found those words rolling around in her brain for a long time.

Crown jewels.

* * *

Their hotel was right on the edge of the area known as the Latin Quarter, a section of the city long associated with higher learning. Alex soaked up all the sights around her as they approached the hotel. Paris had a sense of history that, when seen in person, was almost palpable.

Before they got to the hotel, Alex asked Rachel, "Why's it called the Latin Quarter?"

Without looking at her, Rachel answered, "University students used to go into the shops and restaurants and only speak in Latin. Sort of a 'hey, look at us, we're educated' kind of thing."

"Wouldn't that just come off as really pretentious?"

Rachel chuckled. "Undoubtedly. These *are* college students we're talking about."

After a few moments, Alex said, "Were you pretentious when you were in college?"

That actually made Rachel look around at her. With a mild expression, she said, "Of *course* I was pretentious. I couldn't buck tradition, could I?"

Alex thought they were about to share a laugh, but then Rachel went back to looking out the window, and she spoke clipped French to the cab driver. Alex still couldn't understand a word of their exchange, but Rachel pointed at a modest building coming up on their right, and the meaning was clear: *drop us off there.*

The hotel was tiny compared to most of the corporate monstrosities in America. Alex saw the desk clerk take their key off a pegboard and she quickly counted twenty-six rooms. She decided she liked that. It was kind of cozy.

Her room was also cozy, with a narrow twin bed, a small TV mounted high on one wall, and a tiny bathroom with a quaint pedestal sink. On previous trips, spending all her time in it with mute suits, this room would have been tight and cramped . . . but now, by herself, it couldn't have been more perfect.

She had just finished transferring her clothes from her suitcase to the little dresser near the bed (eyeing them much more critically, in spite of herself, since the whole underwear conversation) when there was a knock at the door. Softly, Rachel's voice came through to her: "You ready to go see a man about a horse?"

Alex opened the door. "I'm sorry?"

Rachel grinned, energetic. "Just something I picked up at the firehouse. C'mon, I know just where to go"—and she peered very theatrically down one end of the hallway, then the other, her voice dropping to a stage whisper—"to find out things about *obscure dead languages.*"

Alex was starting to get very annoyed by Rachel's mood swings.

She checked her watch. Aside from being a proximity sensor, it also kept very accurate time. It was just past three in the afternoon, though it still felt much earlier, thanks to the time zone changes. "Where are we going?"

"To a place I dearly love. Or at least, I dearly love it back home." As they walked down the hallway, Rachel pulled a map of Paris out of her back pocket. "Assuming it's still in the same place . . . ah, yes, it is." She held the map up so Alex could see it, and tapped a spot with one fingernail. "My alma mater. The Sorbonne."

chapter thirteen

Alex didn't know much about the Sorbonne. She was pretty sure it was basically *the* University of Paris, and that the word "prestigious" didn't even begin to describe it. It was one of those places she'd heard mentioned in the kind of hushed, reverential tones reserved for the most famous places on Earth.

As they walked across the campus, passing through a cobblestone square and heading toward a huge, beautiful building that looked like a cross between a cathedral and the Capitol in Washington, Alex couldn't help but ask, "So, you went to the Sorbonne, and now you're a firefighter?"

Rachel grinned a little. "You know what they say. Follow your bliss, right?"

Alex had no response for that. "Um . . . do you know who you're looking for?"

She nodded. "I think so, at any rate. I'm not quite sure what's going to be the same and what's not between home and here, you know? Since *I'm* not the same, I figure there's tons of other stuff that's not either. But I'm hoping that Professor MacMillan won't be too different. And if he's not . . ." She checked her watch. "Okay, let's stay here and wait a minute."

They sat down on a beautiful wrought-iron bench and watched the university students parade by. Alex was both fascinated and thoroughly intimidated.

A lot of these people were her age, she knew, but they seemed a world apart. All of them looked and acted so sophisticated, so confident, so . . . *cool*, though she wished she could think of a better word.

Alex had the option of continuing with classes through the BGO, in the same program that had put her through twelfth grade. She hadn't made up her mind yet; her job was set for life, no matter what, and any more education would just be to better herself, not make her more employable or anything. It wasn't as if she didn't think she needed to learn anything else—quite the opposite. But the thought of several more years of school wasn't exactly thrilling, either.

To go to a place like *this*, on the other hand . . .

She knew she couldn't. Not with what the BGO required of her. But looking around, watching the students in their effortlessly fashionable clothes and their beyond-hip hairstyles . . . God, did she wish she could be one of them.

Her reverie ended when Rachel said, "Hey, there he is!"

Following Rachel's line of sight, Alex saw a small, very bald, very old man with a thick, brushy moustache; he was coming down a set of marble stairs toward them. The man wore old, khaki trousers, brown leather shoes that looked as if they were from World War II, and a battered tweed jacket. He seemed lost in thought.

Alex followed Rachel as she stood and crossed the square toward him.

"Professor!" Rachel called out, lifting a hand.

MacMillan stopped and stared; it seemed to take him a second to focus. "Do I know you, young lady?" he asked warily. "You did want to speak English, I assume?"

Later on, Rachel would provide Alex with a rundown of everything said in this conversation. For now, Alex simply had to stand and listen to the barrage of incomprehensible words that flew back and forth.

In French, Rachel said, "English is my native language, sir, but by no means the only one with which I'm comfortable."

MacMillan glanced around, maybe thinking he could spot some hidden cameras. When he didn't, he gave Alex a careful look, then addressed Rachel—this time in Russian, and with just the hint of a challenge in his eye.

"Not the only one, you say? Perhaps you are familiar with the tongue of the Motherland?"

Rachel chuckled, and in Mandarin Chinese replied, "The Motherland, yes, of course," then switched to Cantonese and finished, "as well as that of their noble neighbors."

Alex shifted her weight from one foot to the other. She felt as if she were witnessing some kind of bizarre nerd duel.

MacMillan began to enjoy it in earnest, though, and had to fight back the laughter when he spoke again, this time in Navajo, "It doesn't take much to learn the common tongues, my dear. If you're trying to impress me you'll have to work much harder."

The air suddenly filled with strange clicks and pops as Rachel answered in the language of the Kalihari Bushmen. "The only question is, how much harder?"

MacMillan's eyes widened, but he didn't lose a step. He spoke in words that very few people alive today had heard pronounced correctly: a dialect of ancient Aztec. "I don't think you understand the rules of the game, my dear. I'm the master here, and if you have even the slightest idea of what I'm saying, raise your left hand."

Rachel's grin got even wider. She raised her left hand in the air—MacMillan didn't even try to hide his astonishment—and then said three distinct words. Alex had never heard anything like them before; they didn't sound like the kinds of things that were supposed to come out of human mouths, and yet they were undeniably words.

The effect on MacMillan was profound. He took a step back, almost staggering, and his voice thudded back into English.

"You . . . you speak Vosarak?"

Rachel shook her head humbly and switched back to English, too. "Only a few words, a phrase here and there. As much as anyone else . . . well, anyone else without access to your resources, sir."

MacMillan rubbed his chest, his eyes still huge. "Who *are* you?"

Rachel stuck her hand out, and while MacMillan shook it weakly, she said, "Come have a cup of coffee with us and I'll tell you."

Half an hour later, the three of them sat around an outdoor table at a small café about a block from their hotel. Alex sipped a café au lait and tried to feel European. The five other tables all seemed to be occupied by university students. Alex was pretty sure most of them recognized the professor, but no one came over to talk.

That was fine with her. The language barrier here felt as high and impenetrable as a prison wall, and Alex knew she would've been reduced to awkward grunts and gestures if anyone had spoken to her. Better that the Parisian students remained apart, so that she could just sort of observe them impartially.

MacMillan continued to speak in English, though, for which Alex was grateful. She could only stay in the dark for so long without going a little nuts.

"My name is Rachel Alexander," Rachel said. She gestured at Alex. "And this is my sister Jeannie. We're tourists, basically, but when I found out we'd be able to come here, I had to look you up."

He shook his head, disbelieving. "You're telling me that you've come this far *on your own?*"

"Well, not on my own, I wouldn't say. I did study all through school, and my Bachelor's degree is in communications."

He waved a hand dismissively. "Yes, yes, but you're saying you've never done any graduate work? Why on Earth not? Why can't I have you in my department, here? Is it money? Do you need me to arrange a fellowship?"

Rachel laughed. "Professor MacMillan, please. I have a job, a career, already." She leaned forward, her voice dropping. "I only came here to ask you a favor."

He frowned. So did Alex; she wasn't sure where Rachel was going with this.

"What sort of favor?"

"Well . . . I know this is irregular, and probably completely unheard of for a non-student, but . . . I was wondering if . . ."

"If? If what? Spit it out, young woman!"

Rachel darted her eyes about as if to make sure no one was listening, then softened her voice to a whisper. "I was wondering if you could let me see the Vosarak Sword. It would mean *so* much to me, just to look at it, just to be in the same *room* with it."

MacMillan slumped back in his chair, the color draining from his face. It was the kind of reaction someone had when they were reminded of an extraordinarily painful memory.

"I'm afraid you've wasted your time this afternoon, my dear." All of MacMillan's feisty intellectualism had abruptly given way to depression and bitter loss.

"Why?" Rachel asked, convincingly sincere. "Would it be *that* much against the rules?"

"Rules have nothing to do with it," MacMillan said, his voice tiny. "The Sword hasn't been here for six months."

"Oh." Rachel's voice held the perfect degree of disappointment. "Was it sent to another university? Or did it go to a museum?"

"The sword was *stolen*." MacMillan sounded as if he were discussing the death of a loved one. "Someone broke into the language department's strongroom and took it."

"Someone *stole* it? But *who*? Who would want to steal something that *unique*? It's not as if you could sell it!"

This confused Alex at first. Why would Rachel pretend not to know the sword had been stolen? But it made sense after she thought about it; the general public didn't even know the sword existed at all, and if she and Rachel had shown up talking about how it had been stolen—something the public *definitely* did not know about—it might have aroused too much suspicion on the professor's part. This way, Rachel just came off as an innocent language enthusiast.

MacMillan shook his head, hopeless. "It's not the theft itself that bothers me so much. It's the *waste*. There are perhaps a handful of people on the planet who can fully appreciate what that sword represents—obviously one more than I was aware of previously—and I know damn well that the thieves are *not* among that number."

Rachel oozed sympathy without saying a word.

"Vosarak is such an unknown quantity," the professor continued. "Yes, we do know something of it, and yes, there is still an oral tradition that allows us knowledge of a tiny portion of its basic pronunciation. But the intricacies of its grammar? The richness of its idioms? All of that was lost, until the sword was discovered. The record of one of Earth's oldest languages, perhaps *the* oldest language, will never be complete now unless it's returned by some cretin who cannot possibly understand what he's stolen."

"Just knowing that Vosarak *had* idioms is beyond my own studies," Rachel said appreciatively.

MacMillan's eyes gained back a bit of their liveliness. He opened his briefcase and rummaged through it, then pulled out a sheet of paper encased in a Mylar sleeve.

"I'm going to show you this," he said. "It's something I've been trying to work out for several years now, and I think I'm close to a breakthrough. I don't know of anyone else who would appreciate it."

He turned the paper around so that Alex and Rachel could see it. Written—or more accurately, drawn—on the page were intricate pictograms including a lot of symbols similar to the ones they had seen on the hologram of the sword.

Reverently, Rachel asked, "What is it?"

"I believe it's a puzzle. An amusement, perhaps." His jaw muscles clenched briefly. "If I had been able to study the sword for just a bit more I could have decrypted it."

"May I—may I have a copy of this?" Rachel asked. MacMillan frowned, and she quickly went on, "You're going to think I'm silly, but I . . . well, I'd sort of like to frame it."

MacMillan laughed. "I'll see if we can't find a copy machine."

They chatted for a few moments more about the pictogram, then Rachel launched into a theory concerning what kind of calendar the speakers of Vosarak may have used, based on the nature of some of the language's proper nouns.

Alex started tuning out.

She knew what Rachel was doing: engaging the professor in a discussion of such detail that he couldn't help but view her as an authority of equal standing. That would make him a good bit more likely to reveal information to her than if she were merely a student, or a dedicated amateur linguist, as she'd first presented herself.

It was just . . . God, it was so *boring*.

Alex Primes were like that a lot of the time. The whole point of them was that they were so supremely specialized in one thing or another that they (in theory) couldn't *help* but succeed. The last one had the market cornered on hostage negotiation; this one knew a billion languages. The one before that had been an expert in sophisticated computer design, and the one before was the theoretical physicist.

And when you're stuck in the back of a van, listening to someone better looking than you and *obviously* about a thousand times smarter, talking endlessly about a subject you have no hope of comprehending, the days drag on at a glacial pace.

Alex took another sip of her coffee. *That* was good, at least. Her eyes wandered around the café, casually taking in the different kinds of people; they seemed to be about as diverse as you'd expect in a public place like this, though she felt pretty sure they were all much cooler than she was.

She glanced over at one young man, sitting alone at a table, reading a book—then her eyes snapped back to him, and she stared for ten full seconds before blushing slightly and looking away for fear he'd glance up and catch her.

He was, without a doubt, what Gail and Chuck would call a "hottie."

Probably in his early twenties. Asian. Maybe Korean, she thought. *I guess that would be Korean-French?* Medium height, very lean . . . his shirt had short sleeves, and when he lifted his own cup of coffee she saw the wiry muscles bunch and ripple in his forearm. And his *eyes*. He darted a look up at the waiter and the light caught them, black and piercing and *oh God, I'm staring again.*

Alex dropped her gaze to her lap and decided to pay attention to the conversation at hand, just in time to hear Professor MacMillan say, "I have quite a large number of research notes, from various projects over the years, that I keep in a small office I rarely use. All of my Vosarak notes are there . . . If you wish to see them."

Rachel projected just the right mixture of humility and eagerness. "Are you . . . are you sure? Since the sword was stolen, wouldn't those notes be, I don't know—*evidence* or something? Don't the police want them?"

MacMillan's eyes were sad. "We're talking about in-depth notes on a language so obscure it makes ancient Incan look like English. The police took one or two peeks at it, realized they'd never be able to make heads or tails of it, and then just let me keep it."

He pulled a business card and a pen out of his jacket pocket, then wrote down an address on the back of the card and handed it to Rachel. "Meet me there in two hours' time. You and your sister, of course. Don't worry, it's not in a bad part of town or anything. I know it's not the same as seeing the sword itself, but perhaps you can learn a bit after all."

Rachel stood, so Alex did too, followed by MacMillan. "Thank you *so* much, Professor," Rachel said. "This is a lot more than I could have asked for."

He shook her hand. "For one as extraordinary as yourself, it is the least I can do."

Alex followed Rachel away from the café, back toward their hotel. As they left, she glanced back to see if the striking young man was still there, reading his book and sipping his coffee.

He wasn't.

Alex sighed and stared at the sidewalk as they went.

chapter fourteen

As Rachel and Alex approached their hotel, a man watched them from inside a shop across the street. As plain and unremarkable as beige wallpaper, he carefully noted their position and destination, then took a small handheld device out of one pocket and popped open a tiny keyboard. His thumbs flashed across the minuscule keys so fast they nearly blurred, and a message appeared on the screen: SUBJECTS SAFE. STILL WATCHING. He hit another button and the message disappeared, sent on its way.

The man slipped the tiny device back into his pocket and continued pretending to look at silk neckties.

* * *

With two hours to kill and nothing specific to do, Alex and Rachel wandered through at least a dozen shops and boutiques. Alex tried to interest Rachel in a lingerie store, since they *were* in Paris and she thought they might at least have a decent conversation about it, but if Rachel had been distant before, now she was practically absent. Her pleasant, soothing manner evaporated completely once they left MacMillan.

Finally Alex couldn't take it anymore, and in as forceful a tone as she could muster (which wasn't terribly forceful), she said, "What's up with you, anyway?"

Rachel blinked vaguely at her. "I'm sorry?"

"You're a million miles away. You're the only person I know here. Can we at least talk a little?"

But Alex could tell, halfway through her last sentence, that Rachel had stopped listening. When she spoke, it was in a halting, distracted fashion shot through with long pauses.

"Sorry, I, uh . . . we'll talk soon, I promise, I just need to think . . . about something . . ."

Alex gave up, beyond frustrated, and followed Rachel in silence as she meandered around the Latin Quarter.

* * *

The sun had just set when Alex and Rachel climbed the front steps of a gray brick building on a quiet Paris street lined with trees Alex didn't recognize. Not that that was saying much; Alex's experience with the great outdoors amounted to zilch, more or less.

Professor MacMillan came shuffling up the sidewalk moments later and called out to them. "I'm glad to see you both made it!" He puffed slightly as he climbed the stairs and passed them, a key in one hand. "I was worried my directions might not have been clear."

"No, no, everything was fine," Rachel said as they followed him inside, bright and attentive again. Alex had begun thinking of that demeanor as Rachel's "game face."

They now stood in a narrow hallway lined with doors; on their left was a stairwell.

"Good." MacMillan gestured toward the stairs. "Come with me; my office is on the second floor. Oh, and here." He pulled a folded sheet of paper out of his jacket pocket and handed it to Rachel. "That photocopy you requested."

Rachel accepted it, and as soon as MacMillan's back was turned, her game face disappeared. She stared at the paper, studying it with a quiet frown, and then seemed to switch to autopilot as she followed the professor.

Alex decided it was time to speak up, even if it was only to ask an inconsequential question. "So, Professor? How come you've got this office if you don't use it? I mean, if all you're going to do here is store things, why not get a storage space?"

MacMillan smiled at her. "An excellent question, young miss." Alex kept her face neutral at the use of the "y" word. "I could indeed simply use a storage unit. But then, if I decided I needed a quiet place to go and think, I'd have to sit on boxes, wouldn't I?"

Before Alex could respond to that rather strange sentiment, MacMillan put an arm out and stopped them both. He stared down the hall and held a shushing finger up to his lips.

Rachel whispered, "What's wrong, sir?"

He pointed to a rectangular shaft of light spilling into the corridor about halfway down. "That's the door to my office," he whispered back. "There appears to be someone inside."

Rachel turned to Alex. "Go back downstairs and call the police." Alex scowled. She knew what Rachel really meant was, *Go someplace where the professor can't see you use your BGO satellite phone, and get Sec or B.C. on the line.* And she was *so* tired of being excluded . . . !

She didn't get the chance to go anywhere. Professor MacMillan said, "No, no, don't separate. If there's a criminal element at work here, we don't want to have the most vulnerable member of our party off by herself." He pulled out his cellular phone. "I'll call the *gendarmes* myself."

But before the professor touched the first number, the office door began to open—slowly, and with a long, nerve-jarring *creak* that raised goose bumps on Alex's arms. Even from this distance, she heard the sound of shuffling feet, moving in an odd, rhythmless pattern . . . and then the *voices.*

Alex glanced up at Rachel and saw from her expression that she'd heard them too. Whoever, or *whatever*, was in that office was *muttering*—a low, chilling, constant sound that made Alex want to scream and run away.

The voices grew louder, and louder still; it was as if a finger had reached straight through Alex's skull and begun scratching at her brain.

The door swung wide, and two shadowy figures stepped out into the hall, both of them carrying large sacks. They were silhouetted, so Alex couldn't make out any details, but suddenly her eyes started watering. There was something *wrong* with those men.

She didn't have time to try to figure out what it was, though, because at that moment the awful muttering began to echo—from *behind* her. She spun, shrieking.

Two more shadowy figures had just followed them from the stairwell into the hallway. They wavered on their feet, as if their joints didn't work quite right, and they muttered in that ghastly way that made Alex want to jam knives in her own ears.

"We don't want any trouble," Rachel said, and then repeated it in French as all four men began to move toward them at a jerking, unsteady pace. Alex, Rachel, and the professor were caught between the two groups with absolutely nowhere to go.

Alex looked at each face, seeing but not really believing. It was that moment that she realized what was wrong with the men.

They looked dead.

More specifically, their skin was pasty white, and their eyes showed only the tiniest sliver of colored irises.

Dead or not, though, they were speeding up.

"Rachel?" Alex said, her voice trembling a bit. "Professor? What do we do?"

"Call for backup!" Rachel answered, her own voice on the rise.

Alex clawed the satellite phone out of her knapsack, but the first of the zombies reached her just then and knocked the phone right out of her hand. Alex screamed as the phone hit the wall and smashed to pieces—in part because the zombies were terrifying, but also because those phones were *expensive*, and in a disconnected sort of way she thought *I'm going to catch hell for that when we get back.*

Then Rachel rushed past her and did something Alex recognized, thanks to Gail's baffling fascination with boxing and no-holds-barred fighting shows: she threw a right hook at the zombie and caught it square in the mouth. The zombie's head rocked back from the force of the blow and a miniature geyser of blood and a couple of teeth exploded from its face, splattering on the nearby wall. It staggered, pouring blood, hands going slowly to its mouth, then its back hit the same wall and it slumped to the floor, motionless.

A horrified but lucid thought flashed through Alex's mind: *These guys aren't dead! Dead guys don't bleed like that. What the hell is wrong with them?*

"Oh, I say!" exclaimed the professor. "Do be careful!"

Rachel was being careful, in point of fact. Confident in her abilities, she hammered the next zombie with four rapid-fire body blows, then finished him off with an uppercut that made his teeth clack together with a sound like a rifle shot.

"The other two are almost here!" Alex cried out, and Rachel turned to face the two who had come from MacMillan's office. Their muttering had changed its timbre—it no longer felt like worms crawling inside Alex's head. All three of them—she, Rachel, and the professor—realized what the zombies were doing.

They were talking to each other.

The words were very low, impossible for her to make out, but Alex thought it sounded like German.

MacMillan clearly had no idea what to do at this point, and Alex wasn't much better off, but Rachel took a few steps toward them, her fists raised. "Whenever you're ready," she said, her words calm and controlled.

The two zombies spoke again, but it was different this time: they both said the same words, as if *chanting*, and the words had the same tone and inflection as the ones Rachel had spoken to Professor MacMillan earlier that afternoon.

Vosarak.

Then the zombies spun on their heels and sprinted down the hallway. Rachel went after them.

God, is she fast, Alex thought.

It only took her a second to reach the slower one. She tackled him, bringing them both down with a tremendous crash. She tried her best to hang on, but the zombie twisted and wriggled like a coyote in a trap. A second later he burst free and followed the other one, flinging himself through an open window at the corridor's far end.

Alex called out, "Are you okay?"

Rachel took a moment to get up, but then she staggered back to Alex and the professor. "Yeah, I'm fine. Slippery bugger." Looking past them, she said, "Ah, damn it."

Alex followed her line of sight and drew in a sharp breath. The first two zombies were gone.

"They must have crept away while you were fighting the other two," MacMillan said, voicing all their thoughts. His theory seemed accurate, especially when Alex noticed the trail of blood spots leading to the stairwell door.

MacMillan looked around at his office, which still stood open. "Well. I suppose I should go in there and ... ahem ... make sure it's empty, yes?"

They followed him, both wary.

Neither Alex nor Rachel was terribly surprised to learn that all of Professor MacMillan's research notes on Vosarak had disappeared. "That must have been what they had in the bags," he muttered, scowling at the file cabinets standing empty in the corner. "Two or three reams' worth of time and effort. Took me *years* to accumulate. All gone."

While MacMillan stood in the center of the office, mumbling to himself and looking around helplessly, Rachel caught Alex's eye, put a finger to her lips for silence, and beckoned to her; Alex followed her out into the hallway. MacMillan didn't notice.

"What's up?" Alex asked in a whisper, her head still spinning, a thought circling in her mind, trying to wiggle its way out.

"We need to go." Rachel glanced at the office. "He'll call the police in a minute, and we probably shouldn't be here when he does."

"You want to just sneak off and leave him? What if those guys come back?"

"Soon as we get outside, I'll call the Bureau. See if they can assign him some protection for a while. Plus I'm sure they'll want to know about the, uh, research-stealing . . . zombified . . . whatever the hell those guys were."

Alex couldn't argue with any of that, so she quietly followed Rachel down the stairs and back out onto the street. Rachel hailed a taxi while she made the call on her satellite phone, and as they climbed inside, the elusive thought finally came to Alex like a wrecking ball to the head.

I COULD HAVE DIED UP THERE!

Alex felt abruptly weak and nauseated, her mouth filled with grainy cotton. She couldn't catch her breath. All her life, on every assignment she'd taken, Alex had always been an observer, and a very indirect one at that. The difference between sitting in the back of an armored van with armed bodyguards and standing in a hallway surrounded by murderous zombified wackos suddenly became painfully clear to her.

It hit her again: *they could have killed me!* And if Rachel hadn't been there, they surely would have. Because what did Alex know about self-defense? Nada. Nil. Zero.

A snippet of conversation came back to her from two years ago, when she mentioned to Sec that Gail had started taking karate, just for fitness, and maybe Alex would like to as well.

"Oh, no, I don't think so," Sec had said with misplaced maternal authority. "Can't take the chance of you rattling that brain around in your skull, can we?"

Alex lolled sideways in the back of the taxi, feeling faint.

"Alex?" Rachel was still on the phone, but she broke the connection and put it away. "You all right?"

"Yeah . . . yeah, I mean, yes, I'm okay—it's just—there were—this wasn't—God, the only reason I could come on this job is that it wasn't supposed to be *dangerous*."

"Ah." One of Rachel's eyebrows twitched upward. She gave the cab driver a quick look to see if he was listening, then said, "Little freaked out, huh?"

Alex nodded. "I mean, I'm sure *your* life is in danger all the time as a firefighter, but this is . . . it's . . . it's just not what I'm used to."

Rachel chuckled. "For what it's worth, if I do my job right, my life *isn't* in danger all the time. It's not like I seek this stuff out."

"But you were so *confident*. You just walked right up and let them have it! What was that? Boxing?"

Rachel shrugged. Alex started to say more, but they arrived at the hotel, and she clambered out while Rachel paid the driver.

They didn't say anything in the elevator; Alex couldn't think of anything intelligent to say, and Rachel didn't seem to want to talk. When they reached their floor, though, Alex tried to continue where they'd left off. "Hey, I know we need to go over what we're doing next—do you, uh, you want to see if we can maybe get a pizza delivered to my room, eat while we talk? I hear they do weird pizzas in France. Put raw eggs on them and stuff."

But when Rachel looked down into Alex's eyes, Alex knew there wouldn't be any more conversation that night. Rachel had the same million-miles-away look she'd had on the flight over.

"Nah, I appreciate it," she said. "But I'm just going to go to my room. I only got halfway through talking to the Bureau, need to finish that up."

And without another word, Rachel sauntered off down the hallway, unlocked her door and disappeared inside. Not a "good night," not a "kiss my butt," nothing.

Alex went to her own room and barely kept herself from slamming the door.

Inside, she sat down on the edge of the bed and reached for her phone. Right now she wanted to talk to someone—*needed* to talk to someone. She could have *died*, for crying out loud, shouldn't she at least *talk* to somebody about that?

Then she remembered. Her phone was in about a thousand pieces, thanks to one of those zombie guys.

The only person she had any real access to right now was Rachel. And Rachel had just shut her door in Alex's face.

Alex went to the tiny refrigerator in the corner, opened it and stared at its contents for two minutes without touching anything, then shut the door again.

She walked over to the desk and picked up the pad of stationery and pen the hotel had provided. She murmured, "Dear Gail and Chuck," then sat down, and wrote the letter *D* at the top left corner of the first sheet, hesitated, then laid both the pad and the pen back down.

She got down on the floor and did forty sit-ups. That didn't help either. *Nothing* helped.

Finally, feeling as if her insides were about to boil out of her ears, Alex cracked her door and peered up and down the hall. There was no one there—no Rachel, no other guests, no one. She checked her watch; according to the proximity sensor, Rachel was still in her room, doing God knew what.

And instead of staying freaked out and scared, Alex's emotions tipped over into something she had a lot of experience with: quiet, repressed anger. Except now that anger might not be so repressed anymore. Her hands gripped the edge of the door until her knuckles turned white.

Rachel didn't want to talk?

Fine. There had to be *somebody* in Paris who spoke English.

With a sense of defiance that up to this point she had considered only in the abstract, Alex closed and locked her door, then headed for the lobby. She was pretty sure B.C. would have a full-blown seizure if he found out about this. But B.C. wasn't there, was he?

No one stopped her as she crossed the lobby. No one stopped her as she stepped outside onto the street and took a deep breath of night air. Feeling anxious, but enjoying the evening more with each passing moment, Alex turned right and started walking toward the café where she and Rachel had had coffee with Professor MacMillan.

chapter fifteen

The crowd was light at the café; only two of the five outdoor tables had people at them. Sitting alone, she felt like some kind of impostor, as if someone were just about to come up and say, "I'm sorry, you aren't allowed to be here, please go back to your room."

But the only person who approached her was the waiter. Glancing at the menu, she managed to speak the three words of French she felt sure of, and even then she mentally kicked herself for not *sounding* sure at all. "Café au lait?"

The waiter nodded curtly and left. Alex tapped one foot, looking around, trying to relax . . . and then her throat clamped down on her next breath like a vice. She had to make a serious effort to inhale, because the sleekly handsome young Asian man she'd seen that afternoon had just arrived at a table adjacent to hers, not five feet away. He set his book on the table, pulled his chair out, glanced around casually . . .

And this time he *did* catch her staring.

To Alex's simultaneous exhilaration and bafflement, he smiled at her before turning to the approaching waiter.

Alex's heart rate skyrocketed. Grasping for something to focus on so that her head didn't float completely off her shoulders, she squinted at the book in the young man's hand, the same one he'd been reading earlier: it was *Slaughterhouse-Five*, by Kurt Vonnegut.

Oh my God! she thought. *I've read that!*

Suddenly it became important, for some reason she couldn't quite grasp, not to look at the young man. She made a study of her fingernails, then the irregularities of the surface of the table, then the toes of her shoes. Anything but him!

Then the waiter came back with her drink, and in the process of handing him her money, Alex's eyes darted toward the young man again. Just as her gaze flashed across him he looked up and made eye contact with her—and then it was too late.

Caught like the proverbial deer in headlights, Alex smiled and gave him the lamest little wave possible.

He grinned, an easy, comfortable grin, displaying perfect, brilliant white teeth. "You're American, aren't you?"

He had a pleasant voice, even-toned, his words flavored with a French accent that made her stomach flip-flop. It took her a second or two to respond.

"How—how did—?"

"How did I know?" He put a bookmark in the Vonnegut book and set it back on the table, turning his attention fully to her. "We have a few American tourists in this city, you might say. You tend to have a certain look about you." His smile was so . . . she didn't want to say *dazzling*, that was so cliché, but what other word was there? "My name is David." He pronounced it *Dah-veed*. "What might yours be?"

Alex's head spun for the second time that night. She felt so divorced from reality that she imagined herself stepping aside from this scene, watching it, and commenting like a narrator.

Let's tick off the reasons why your mouth is stuffed with cotton right now, she said to herself. The Alex in conversation with David sat obligingly frozen in place so that narrator-Alex could lean over and speak into her ear. *Number one, you're not supposed to be here, and you're so tense you think your tongue's about to fall out.*

Number two, you're in a city jammed so full of gorgeous women—Rachel among them—that your ordinarily low self-esteem has pretty much bottomed out.

And number three—the most important one, let's keep that in mind. Number three is that you've never even held hands with a boy before, much less had a boyfriend!

What the hell are you doing talking to this guy who you don't know from Adam?

"Alex." She was a little surprised to hear the word leave her lips. "My name's Alex."

"Alex? Isn't that a boy's name?"

She blushed a little and looked down again. "It's short for Alexandra."

"I see." A slight pause, then, "Did I notice you looking at the book?" He tapped the Vonnegut.

Alex nodded. Something to talk about besides herself! "I, yes, I did, I was—I've read it. Studied it, actually, ah, in class."

David's smile became, if possible, even more enthralling. He glanced around, looking for the waiter, then said, "If you would not mind—that is, if you are here alone—perhaps you would not mind if I joined you?"

The waiter approached again, this time bringing David's coffee. With her narrator voice chattering in her ear to the tune of *Who are you and what have you done with Alex Benno?* Alex said, "I'd be delighted."

"Very good." He stood, took his coffee from the waiter, and sat down quite gracefully in a chair across from her. On some nearly subconscious level, she appreciated that. If he had sat right next to her it would have been too much.

For half an hour, Alex and David chatted, mostly discussing *Slaughterhouse-Five*; she had written a paper on it, and was delighted to find that he shared her opinion of what had happened to the reality-challenged main character. At first, she feared her nerves would mangle anything interesting or intelligent that she might think to say, but to her continued surprise and unabashed delight, she found herself talking quite naturally. She was even, she thought, a little charming.

It was very much like being dropped into a deep pool for the first time and discovering she could tread water.

Alex had drawn a breath and opened her mouth to ask, "So where did you grow up?" when she saw David glance at something over her shoulder. His face changed, darkening, his smile fading quickly.

"What is it?" she asked, and started to follow his line of sight.

"No, no, don't look," he said. "Please face me." She realized he had moved slightly, putting her in between him and whatever it was he had seen.

Growing alarmed, Alex whispered, "What's wrong? What's going on?"

David sighed, and spoke reluctantly. "It's my ex-girlfriend, Babette. She won't stop following me."

Alex's eyebrows slowly rose. She couldn't decide how she felt about this new wrinkle, but her interest certainly didn't fade. Still whispering, Alex asked, "Where is she?"

He looked at the ground. "Over your left shoulder, about fifteen meters back."

Slowly, as casually as she could, Alex turned and risked a look. Standing at the far edge of the café's property, a young woman with wavy blonde hair perused a freestanding chalkboard with the day's menu written on it.

Alex's heart dipped a little; she had no doubt that this was Babette (of *course* her name was Babette) . . . and Babette was *very* pretty. Slender but strong, like a volleyball player, with tanned skin and full, red lips.

Alex's newfound confidence began a swift, steep decline. She'd never felt mousier or less attractive.

But that feeling changed abruptly as she felt David's hand close gently on her wrist. "I think she will probably want to talk if she sees me," he said softly, leaning in close to her, his breath warm and soft against her cheek. "Would you like to walk with me? Away from this place? From *her?*"

Alex looked into his eyes, eyes as black and deep as the midnight ocean, and she forgot completely about everyone else. "Let's go."

* * *

Standing under a streetlight at the nearest corner, the same unremarkable man who had observed and reported on Alex and Rachel earlier watched as Alex passed by with David. They didn't look at him—no one ever did—and all but the most diligent of observers would have missed his furtive but penetrating glances at them. The man waited until they had been gone for a full minute, then strolled after them.

But even as skilled as he was, the unremarkable man didn't notice one shadow among many others as he walked past a dim alleyway; neither did he notice the thin nylon cord that shot out of the darkness and looped around his neck.

His surveillance came to an abrupt end, marked only by the soft, receding sound of his heels dragging across the pavement.

* * *

Fifteen minutes later, Alex walked with David beside the River Seine, marveling at the stunning and welcome turn her night had taken.

He hadn't touched her, other than that brief, light grasp of her wrist at the café. Yet he walked very close to her, and she could feel the warmth of his skin.

They chatted further, the conversation still easy, natural. Comfortable. Alex enjoyed hearing his voice, no matter what he was saying, but she listened attentively as he talked about his childhood and what led him to become a student at the Sorbonne.

"My father wanted me to go into computers." He picked up a pebble and tossed it toward the river; it skipped across the water three times before sinking. "But languages have always been my first love, and I don't think there's any better place to study them than here."

"I have a friend who's very much into languages," Alex said, then wished she hadn't. She'd intended not to mention Rachel at all.

David smiled. "Is that the tall woman you were with earlier?"

"You, uh . . . you saw us?"

He faced her as they came to a stop, his smile warm and comforting. "You *saw* me see you."

"Well, I . . . I didn't think you were, y'know, paying *attention.*"

David calmly reached out and took her hands in his. "May I make a confession?" Alex nodded mutely, staring up into his eyes again. "I did want to go out tonight to get away from Babette. But I went to that specific café . . . on the tiny chance that I might see you there again."

Alex pulled her hands away. "You're making that up."

He shook his head, but didn't get any closer. He seemed to know exactly how to maintain a non-threatening distance between them. "Why would I? I saw you, and wanted to know more of you."

Alex sputtered. Then—she knew she shouldn't say this, but she couldn't help it— "Why were you looking at *me*? Didn't you see who was sitting next to me? I mean, come *on* . . . we looked like a before-and-after picture."

He moved the tiniest bit closer.

"Alex . . . I did not wish to know you better for your appearance alone. But for as much as it is worth? I find you graceful. Elegant. Like the gazelle. Not like these overly developed Western women. Your friend, she is quite . . . What is the word? Curvaceous."

Alex narrowed her eyes at him, skeptical. "Curvaceous, that's one word for it."

David lightly, so lightly, ran one fingertip down her arm to her hand. "You are prettier than she."

Are you kidding me?!

Alex turned away, looking everywhere except at David. They had entered a small, beautiful park area, and maybe fifty feet away stood a small building with some public restrooms.

"Excuse me," she said, and headed toward the one with the stylized picture of a person wearing a skirt.

He took a step after her. "Are you all right?"

"I'm fine, I'm fine, I just . . . just give me a minute, all right? Just wait; wait right there, I'll be right back."

From behind her she heard him say, "Okay," his voiced tinged with confusion.

Once inside—the place was relatively small, with two stalls and two sinks—Alex went to the farthest sink from the door, turned on the faucet, and splashed some cold water on her face. She stared into the mirror above the sink for a few seconds, then whispered, "You're not even wearing makeup."

What looked like a frightened young girl stared out at her. Mouse-brown hair so curly it was almost kinky, skin so pale you could practically see through it, washed-out blue eyes, a nose as boring as dust, lips that she suspected were too thin to be good for kissing.

Not that she knew from personal experience.

This night is magical . . . isn't it?

Or is it too good to be true? What if David does this all the time? What if he plans to charm me back to his room, or slip something into my drink if we stop at another café?

Why is he giving me the time of day in the first place?

Nice, the narrator said in her mind. *Try to be as cynical as possible. Don't give yourself even the tiniest shred of credit. Nobody could possibly be attracted to you; you're worth less than dirt.*

Blue eyes staring into blue eyes, Alex said aloud, "What am I *doing?*"

Then she noticed something in the mirror: one of the stall doors had moved. Maybe half an inch.

Before she could get a word out, the door crashed open in a whirlwind of blonde hair and tan skin. Babette said, "Lights out," and then everything did indeed get very dark.

chapter sixteen

Sonnet Ivandrova's parents left Moscow when Sonnet was barely three years old.

Their beliefs and values had already put them at risk. When their tiny daughter began . . . making *things* happen . . . they knew they would have to flee. Somewhere far away. Some place where no one would point fingers and whisper about the little girl who could make birds fall dead from the sky just by looking at them.

They settled in London, and there Sonnet grew up. At age five, she gained control over the qualities that made her unique, and so was able to attend a fine boarding school without worry of giving herself away.

But her visits home reinforced what her parents had taught her to believe, what she didn't question: that black magic should be the true force of order on Earth. It had been demonstrated by Rasputin, the visionary monk who came close to seizing power over the pre-Soviet Russian government. The mission now lay with Sonnet's parents and Sonnet herself: to see the skulls of the masses cracked open and Rasputin's message poured inside.

Upon graduating from university, Sonnet worked for one year as a freelance assassin. Her services were in high-demand, since her jobs *always* looked like accidents. (What assassin could cause eight tons of rock to break loose from a cliff face and crush a visiting ambassador's passing car? Police investigations revealed no explosives or other artificial agents involved. Just a tiny fault in the stone that simply picked that instant to give way.)

She had just begun finalizing with her parents the list of government heads to eliminate when she was contacted by Baron Giacomo Morbidini. The Baron offered her a more sound, far-reaching plan for the world than any she had seen.

And Morbidini took her dark agenda into consideration. Not just that; he *counted* on it. Sonnet pledged her loyalty to the Baron's creation of the Sacred Knights of Altered Reality, and immediately set about helping him achieve his shadowy goals.

As Alex Benno whirled from the mirror, several hundred miles away, Sonnet Ivandrova and the Gray Baron stood in a long, rectangular room, staring at the Vosarak Sword through a thick layer of bulletproof glass.

"It feels right," Sonnet said quietly.

The Baron glanced at her. Sonnet heard the soft metallic whisper as his head swiveled on his neck. "What do you mean?"

"This marriage. Magic and technology." She met his eyes. "Every line of code, every word in the ancient language. All of it, imbued with my power, the power of my mother and father, the power of those who came before them. In no other way could our message be heard by so many people in so short a time."

"The world will thank you," the Baron answered. His eyes went back to the sword. "They will bow before us, and they will look up and thank us all."

"I've had my eye on someone for a while," Sonnet said, after a contemplative pause. "A young woman in California named Amy Titus."

"Yes?"

"I think she might have some genuine psychic ability. Have your men pick her up, would you? I would love to discover whether Vosarak can augment extrasensory talent."

"Consider it done."

Sonnet stretched like a cat, then glanced dispassionately at the crumpled, bloodstained heap of flesh on the floor behind them, barely recognizable as human.

"Remind me who that was?" she asked.

"His name was Slotnick." A note of distaste crept into the Baron's voice. "I had just finished with him when you arrived."

"Ah." She nodded. "One of theirs, then?"

"Mine. His performance was substandard. Though I believe he ultimately proved a source of great inspiration to his coworkers."

* * *

Alex awakened with an awful pounding in her head and sharp burning pain in her wrists and ankles. The world slowly shifted into focus around her: she sat in a chair, her arms and legs tied to the frame; she was in what she thought must be a small, empty storage room. She couldn't tell how long she'd been out.

The one thing she was sure of, as her stomach twisted into knots, was that she was scared out of her mind.

"I'm surprised you're awake so soon," said a feminine voice from behind her. Her accent sounded French, but very different from David's.

Alex made a pained sound as the pretty blonde woman called Babette moved into her field of vision. "Most people take longer to recover from one of my nerve strikes."

"Where am I?" Alex asked weakly. The sound of her own voice made her head pound harder.

"That's not important," Babette said. "What's important is how you and I communicate right now." She knelt beside Alex. "I'm willing to do it the easy way, if you want. I'd much prefer that. I don't really enjoy the alternative."

Even though her throat wanted to seal tight, Alex managed to squeak, "I don't know what you're talking about."

Babette frowned. "All right, now you're trying my patience. But I'll give you the benefit of the doubt, in case you're not as awake as you seem to be." She stood, grabbed Alex's hair and cranked her head painfully backward. Then she leaned over so that their eyes were no more than three inches apart. Alex gasped, tried to twist away, but couldn't.

"You work for the American government," Babette said, her voice barely above a growl now. "You are here because of a computer virus recently discovered. It has something to do with a dead language called Vosarak. And you're going to tell me everything you know, not only about the virus, but also . . . about . . . *yourself*."

She released Alex's hair. Her head slumped forward, and tears came in a torrent as Alex started sobbing.

Was this what her whole life had been leading up to? Her first real taste of freedom, and she'd been taken prisoner *immediately*?

Or was this happening because she'd dared to think for a few minutes that somebody might be attracted to her?

As the sobbing grew worse, shaking her whole body, Alex could see the report: *Operative Alex Benno, captured and interrogated on first mission. Security compromise: maximum. Resulting value of operative: nil.*

"Oh, good God," Babette said. "Let us not waste time like this, all right? You are the best actress, all right? You can stop the crying."

Alex squinted up at her through the tears and saw that she held a large hypodermic needle in one hand.

But that wasn't what struck Alex the most. What hit home with unexpected clarity was that this woman, Babette, thought Alex was faking it.

And before that thought could sink in any deeper, the door to the storage room burst completely off its hinges and slammed to the floor a few feet to Alex's right.

Babette jumped, startled, but she made no sound. Somehow she swapped the hypodermic for a long, thin, wicked-looking knife, just as Rachel came through the doorway in a rush, her upper lip curled into a determined snarl.

The two women met right in front of Alex, who was desperately trying to scoot her chair backward.

She had never seen two people move faster in her life. Even as she rocked the chair and pushed with her toes, she couldn't really follow the individual movements. The silver of the knife blade flashed for two seconds, maybe three, then it somehow jumped from Babette's hand and thudded into the ceiling point-first. Babette and Rachel circled each other for half a second more, then Rachel sped forward and landed a punch straight to Babette's chin. Then she dealt another one.

Babette moved with the blows, twisted to one side and delivered a punishing kick to Rachel's ribs, forcing her to take a staggering step backward. Babette darted to the left—and then dashed out the door, gone in a split second.

Rachel panted a little. She straightened up and turned to Alex.

And Alex knew what Rachel saw: a pitiful, useless little girl, bound hand and foot, her face stained with tear streaks.

There was no judgment in Rachel's expression, not yet. She simply said, "Let's get you out of this," and began untying the ropes, which had cut into Alex's wrists and ankles.

Alex kept quiet while Rachel freed her. Rachel seemed aware that Alex didn't want to talk, so neither of them spoke as Rachel led her out of the storage room. They emerged onto the sales floor of what appeared to be an out-of-business flower shop, and seconds later they reached the street. Alex looked around until she saw a sign with a familiar street name. *That runs past the hotel.* She sniffled once and started walking toward it, wiping at her nose and her face.

Rachel fell in step next to her. "Are you all right?"

And that was it. With hot tears burning her eyes again, Alex whirled on Rachel and shouted, "What do you *think?* Am I all *right?* Get the hell *away* from me!"

Rachel's eyes got huge for a second, then narrowed. "Now, hold on a second," she began.

"Just leave me *alone!*" Alex screamed, then turned and ran, determined to put as much distance between herself and Rachel as she possibly could.

Alex had reached the corner and turned toward the hotel before Rachel caught up with her, but Rachel ran like a damn cheetah. Alex thought Rachel probably just let her have those few seconds of a lead.

Now Rachel put a hand on Alex's shoulder and stopped her. There was no question of Alex being able to resist Rachel's strength, so she didn't try. "I said hold on a second. Just listen to me, okay?"

Alex violently shrugged out of Rachel's grasp and glared up at her sullenly. "What, what, what do you want?"

"It's not what I want." Her voice stayed very calm and measured, but it had an edge to it that Alex hadn't heard before.

She was pretty sure Rachel was furious with her. "It's what I need. I need to talk to you. I think I've figured something out."

"All right. Go ahead, talk."

Rachel glanced around. "Not here. Back in my room. There's something there you should see."

Quiet, sulking, Alex followed Rachel back. The hotel's lobby was deserted except for one loud American tourist complaining about his lousy cell phone reception. The desk clerk being yelled at blithely pretended not to speak English.

In Rachel's room, she motioned for Alex to have a seat at the tiny breakfast table in the corner while she closed the door. Then she came and sat down on the edge of the bed and fixed Alex with a clear, steady look.

"I'm not going to go into the hows and whys of what you were doing out there," she began.

Alex rolled her eyes, still seething. She was furious at Babette and more so at David, but most of all she was angry with herself.

Rachel continued as if she hadn't noticed. "I'm just going to assume you're aware of the causes and repercussions and say it's a lesson learned. Okay?"

Alex glared at Rachel. This was so typical; Alex Prime never loses her temper, always has some smart, mature thing to say. Alex was so incredibly sick of it. She was sick of everything: sick of Rachel and all the others like her. Sick of the BGO. Sick of her own warped, stunted life that demanded she suffer so other people could be helped. Why? Why did *she* have to be the one to suffer? Why couldn't it be somebody else? *Anybody* else?

"So you don't have anything else to say to me?" Alex couldn't keep her voice from trembling. "That's it, huh? *Don't do it again, that's sufficient?*"

Rachel shrugged. "What do you want from me? You want me to scold you? Punish you? Number one, I think you're plenty intelligent enough to know how dangerous and boneheaded it was to go off like that. Number two, I'm not your mother. Number three, we don't have the time."

"What, are you saying you haven't already reported this to Sec?"

"Even if I were inclined to, which I'm not particularly." She pointedly held up her satellite phone. "This isn't working. Is yours?"

Frowning, Alex said, "Mine got totaled back at the professor's office, so you're—" *Hang on a minute.* "Yours isn't working? For real? That's . . . that's not even supposed to be *possible.* I mean, that's the whole point of those things, that they work anywhere."

She started to say something else, then suddenly remembered the tourist in the lobby with the bad cell phone reception. The cloud of anger over her head began to dissipate a tiny bit, replaced by mounting confusion. "What's going on?"

"I think it's the Vosarak virus," Rachel said, her tone grim. "I think it's a multi-stage thing, and right now it's targeting communications. We're just lucky it hasn't affected our proximity sensors, or I wouldn't have known where to find you once I realized you weren't in your room."

"Oh yeah? Why were you looking for me?" Even as the gravity of the situation started to sink in, Alex couldn't help lashing out. She'd been sitting on this hurt for a while. "It's not like you wanted to *talk* to me, is it?"

Sudden understanding blossomed in Rachel's face. "Oh— oh! Oh, Alex. Look, it's not that I didn't want to talk to you, okay? I just—on the flight over here, I'd been thinking about all this stuff, with Vosarak used in the computer virus and putting *that* together with the research I'd been doing back home, and something occurred to me. Like all in a flash, y'know? I've just had to take time to work it out in my mind. That's why I've been so head-in-the-clouds. It wasn't because of *you*."

Alex couldn't tell which way was up. The pure, abject humiliation she felt for going out and getting captured like a . . . only one word came to mind for what she'd done. Like a *dumbass*. And to be rescued by Rachel! Of *course*, the first time in her life she got in serious trouble, of *course* the one woman who made her feel the most like dirt came riding in like the cavalry.

But now Rachel was apologizing, more or less.

Plus she hadn't yelled at her *much*.

Alex squeezed her eyes shut for a moment and said, "Okay, well . . . what was it? What was this thing you realized?"

Rachel took a deep breath and surprised Alex once again by looking faintly embarrassed. "This is going to sound nuts, but considering how you brought me here from another *dimension*, I'll assume your mind is more open than most."

Alex's forehead wrinkled. "Oookay . . ."

"Here goes, and I'm just going to come out and say it: I don't think Vosarak started out on Earth. I think it's a relic of ancient contact with extraterrestrials."

chapter seventeen

Dead silence.

Alex thought she might have heard herself blink.

"Ex*cuse* me?"

"I know, I know, it's crazy, but hear me out." Rachel took another deep breath. "Vosarak's been around forever, but nobody knows where it came from. Examples have been found in wildly varying geographical locations, like on opposite sides of the planet, and thousands of years ago travel wasn't exactly easy. Plus what really convinced me were those wackjob zombie guys outside Professor MacMillan's office. They spoke in Vosarak!"

Alex struggled with this. "Yeah . . . ? So? So they spoke in Vosarak, so what?"

"I think—this is hard to say, because it scares the crap out of me, thinking about what it could mean—I think Vosarak can be used as part of a virus that affects not only computers and electronics, but also the human mind."

Alex sat back in her seat, scowling. "Oh, come *on*. What are you *talking* about? Affect the human mind *how?*"

"Well . . . I think I can prove it to you."

"You're kidding."

Rachel's expression didn't change.

"You're *not* kidding. Okay, yes. Show me. This I've got to see."

Rachel went over to the small table beside the bed and picked up a piece of paper. Alex could see something written on it, but from that angle she couldn't tell what. Rachel came back and sat down, four or five feet away from Alex.

"I'm going to show this to you."

"Okay?"

"And then I want you to tell me how you feel."

"All right. Show me your magic brain-drain words."

Rachel flipped the piece of paper around and held it up. It was another pictogram, but nowhere near as complex as the one MacMillan had shown them. And yet . . . there was something about it—as Alex stared, and couldn't *stop* staring, the twisting, flourished symbol grew more vivid and her eyes widened . . . and then Alex could have been standing in the middle of an orange grove, the scent was so strong.

Right there, out of nowhere, she certainly hadn't been thinking about *oranges* of all things, but the *scent*, the scent filled her nostrils, filled her head, rich and biting and so powerful she couldn't—

Rachel dropped the paper.

Alex slumped in her chair. She almost fell out of it, then jumped up and backed away. "What . . . the *hell* . . . was *that?*"

Rachel stayed calm, but her shoulders had tensed up. "What was it that you felt?"

Alex looked around, not quite hysterical. "Oranges! I smelled *oranges!*"

Rachel nodded, laid the paper facedown on the bed. "That was just one word, Alex. What I just showed you. I've been studying Vosarak for years back home, you know that, right? Well, a couple of years ago I found this one symbol, and whenever I looked at it for a long time, I thought I could smell oranges. So faint I thought I was imagining it. At first, anyway.

"So when I started thinking about it all *here,* with the computer virus, and then especially when MacMillan showed me that pictogram, things started to click into place a little more. I took that copy he gave me and cross-referenced it with my 'orange' symbol, and I saw where I'd made a couple of mistakes, so I re-drew it, got it a lot more accurate. And you just experienced the result. That one word in Vosarak *affected your mind*, Alex. That one word made you think you were smelling oranges."

Alex leaned against the wall, mostly to keep from falling down. "So—so, wait, if you did that with one word . . ."

Rachel's voice trembled a little. "My understanding of Vosarak is pretty damn good. Better than anybody's, really, at least back home. But it's not perfect. It couldn't be perfect, not without something to fill in the blanks. Something to act as a translation key."

"Something like the sword," Alex breathed. "With the sword, SKAR can totally master the whole language, can't they?"

"And if I can get into your head the way I did with just one word, imagine what they could do if they were fluent in it."

Alex shuddered.

"So here's the situation," Rachel went on. "Our communications are getting scrambled. I don't know if that's just localized or nationwide or global or what, but I think I know where the sword is."

"Huh?" Alex hadn't seen *that* coming. "How?"

"Those two zombies, back at the professor's office? One of them said a name. *The Gray Baron.*"

Alex groaned. "Great. But how does that let you know where the sword is?"

Rachel managed a strained grin as she reached into a pocket and pulled out a man's leather wallet. "It doesn't. But I lifted this off the zombie I tackled. Guy's a security guard at an art museum in Berlin. I've got his ID card and everything."

"*What?* Why didn't you tell me you took the guy's *wallet?*"

Rachel shrugged. "I didn't know if it was going to be helpful or not. Plus, y'know, it was kind of . . . well . . . *larcenous.*"

Alex laughed involuntarily.

Rachel went on. "I did some checking, and I think the museum's a pretty likely candidate. The way it's set up, they could have anything down in the lower levels and keep it really secure. Plus . . . those zombie guys. This is just a theory, but I think they're some kind of, I don't know, some kind of *side effect*. I can't imagine anybody would deliberately make people act like that. I mean, yeah, they're *weird*, but I wouldn't call them *effective*."

Alex sighed, long and heavy. "Okay . . . so . . . let me try and sum up here. SKAR has this language that can affect computers *and* people, they want to use it to follow through with their plans of global ass-kicking, they've probably already started doing it, and we're the only two people on the planet who know what they're doing and maybe have a chance to stop it."

Rachel nodded. She sat down on the edge of the bed and leaned forward, her elbows on her knees, plaintive.

"Alex . . . I know you don't want anything to do with this. I know you don't want anything to do with *me*. But we've got no backup now. Thanks to this communications thing, we're out in the cold. And we have to work together if we're going to do it at all. I need you. And I know this sounds like a line from some movie or something, but it's the truth: the *world* needs you. Will you help me?"

Maybe it was Rachel's voice, or her choice of words, or maybe even her body language, but things suddenly started to sink in with Alex in a big way. The enormity of the situation loomed in front of her like a boulder rolling steadily toward her, about to crush her.

"Oh . . . God," Alex said. She slid down the wall until she was sitting on the floor, her eyes abruptly vacant. "This is—this is *it*. This is real . . . this is the whole *world*?"

Rachel nodded again. "Yeah, I think it is. More important,"— and these next words went off like sticks of dynamite in Alex's brain—"it's *your* world."

With a violent wrenching of perspective, Alex realized how tiny, how insignificant her personal issues were when compared with the global terror that would descend if SKAR's virus did its job. *How selfish*, she thought. *How immature.*

Slowly, Alex stood, then looked around her as if seeing the world through a whole new pair of eyes.

"Okay," she said, her voice even. "Okay. I guess we should get going then, huh?"

* * *

It didn't take them long to rent a car. The BGO had supplied them with an abundance of traveler's checks, and the hotel clerk was more than happy to wake up the necessary people once Rachel had slipped him a couple hundred euros.

Sitting very close to each other in the tiny European car, they headed out onto the highway, pointed north. Next stop, Germany.

Rachel lapsed back into a silence, but it didn't have the "I'm-ignoring-you" hostile nature that Alex had perceived before. Alex was glad of the quiet this time; in fact, it gave her ample opportunity to process everything that had happened in the last several hours. She slid the moonroof cover back, leaving the glass in place, and stared, unfocused, up at the night sky above them.

Her emotions had run the gamut from ecstasy at the attention David paid her, to the most crushing sensation of uselessness and despair she'd ever felt, to a sort of thunderous shock at having the power of Vosarak demonstrated in a very personal way. It was that last one that had the most lasting effect.

It's a matter of perspective, she said to herself. Rachel had a job to do. And it was up to Alex to make sure she could do it.

"Y'know, I've been on a lot of assignments," Alex said, breaking the silence.

Rachel glanced over at her. "Yeah?"

"Yeah. But none like this. If you hadn't figured this out . . . well, I don't really want to think too much about it. I'm just—I mean, what I'm trying to say is—I, uh, I'm glad you're here. To pull our fat out of the fire, I mean."

Rachel chuckled. "I know what you're saying, about trying not to think too much about it. I've been failing at that for the last twelve hours. Listen, I'm happy to help, but I think you're missing the point about who's to thank if we can pull this off."

". . . Huh?"

"Look, if a scientist invents a robot that can go into burning buildings and save people's lives, and then the robot goes and rescues a bunch of orphans, who deserves the thanks there? The robot?"

Alex frowned, but didn't answer.

Rachel continued, "No, of course not. The scientist is the one responsible. Get what I'm saying? *You're* the one who's saving the world, Alex. You brought me here. Without you, your whole planet would fall prey to these SKAR people."

Alex shook her head, resistant to the idea. "It's not me, though. It's never me. I can't do any of these things. You're the reason we'll be able t—"

Rachel cut her off. "Just mull that over for a while, okay? What I said, all right? And think of it this way, too: if you had a treasure chest filled with all the riches in the world, but it was locked . . . what would really be worth more? The treasure chest? Or the key?"

Alex sat there, silent, trying to come up with something to say. Rachel didn't give her the chance, though. "Moving right along, I want to teach you something."

"Huh? Teach me—What?"

"Some words in Vosarak. If SKAR is messing with people's minds already, and it sure as hell looks like they are, I want to teach you some words that might counteract the effects if they try to do it to you."

"Uh . . . okay . . . but I have to tell you, with you being around, my foreign language skills have dropped to *nothing*. I'm not even that confident in my ability to speak *English* anymore."

"It's okay, you don't really have to understand what they mean. I just want you to learn them phonetically."

"Well . . . yeah, all right. Hit me."

Rachel made a sustained noise that sounded to Alex like a cross between a garage door opening and a monkey howling.

"Oh, there is *no way* I'm going to be able to learn that!"

Rachel smiled patiently. "Sure you can. I mean, we'll be driving all night, what else are you going to do?"

"Ugh. Okay . . . let me hear it again." Rachel made the sounds once more, and Alex did her best to imitate them.

"Not bad," Rachel said, pleased. "You're getting there."

Alex was less than convinced, but tried it again, and this time Rachel said she was even closer.

"And what's this supposed to do? Keep them from taking over my mind or something?"

"Yeah." Rachel smirked a little. "That, or give you a brain aneurysm. One or the other."

Alex blinked. "You're kidding. You *are* kidding, right?"

Rachel grinned broadly. "Let's try it again, shall we?"

"*Tell* me you're kidding!"

chapter eighteen

The next day proved to be both reassuring and unsettling; reassuring in that Alex and Rachel made contact with Sec, and unsettling in that the communications blackout seemed to be narrowing its focus.

They had entered Germany and were heading toward Berlin, home of the Steinholz Museum, where Rachel suspected the Vosarak Sword was being kept. Alex had been checking Rachel's satellite phone every half hour or so, and she tried it again, not really expecting to get any results.

She let out a yelp when the signal went through.

"Where are you?" Sec's voice demanded without preamble. "Give me your location immediately!"

Alex hit the button to switch to speaker phone.

"We're about ten kilometers outside Berlin," Rachel said, keeping her eyes on the road but turning her head a little toward the phone.

"Are you injured? Are you both all right?"

"We're fine," Alex answered. She even grinned a little at Rachel when she said it.

"There's a small private airfield just inside Berlin's city limits," Sec said, talking rapidly. "Kohler Air Charters. Get there and we'll send agents to extract you—"

And then the signal went dead, the phone's screen fading to static.

Alex looked over at Rachel. "How come it worked just then? Why now, why here, when it hasn't worked all night?"

Rachel frowned thoughtfully and didn't answer for a minute. "I can think of a couple of reasons. One, SKAR's interference isn't as great as we thought, and the signal can get through every now and then, like cloud cover breaking."

"You don't sound like you believe that."

Rachel shook her head. "I don't. I think we might've gotten out of the interference's range as it was expanding, though. Here, let me check something." She turned on the car's radio, and a strong station came through, an announcer chattering in German. Rachel frowned.

"What does that mean?"

"I think it means the interference has *narrowed*. They don't want to freak out the entire country—or, I guess at this point it would be the entire world—if a big chunk of Europe suddenly had a long-term, unexplained communications blackout."

"Okay . . . ?"

"I think they've narrowed it specifically to prevent people like us from using encrypted satellite signals."

"So . . . oh, God—do you think they know we're coming?"

Rachel shrugged. "Beats me." She looked Alex in eye. "I'm not a spy, y'know. I'm pretty tough, I can put out a house fire with the best of them, and I have a gift for languages. But, correct me if I'm wrong, this wasn't supposed to be you and me in the middle of some big international incident. This was just supposed to be you and me talking with a few academic types and trying to figure out where to tell the BGO to look."

Alex nodded grimly. "You're not wrong."

"So now the Bureau knows where we're headed, but it's not like they can send a bunch of troops into Germany and grab us up. Not with your global political climate the way it is right now. Probably not ever. The best they could do would be to try and mobilize some other covert types."

"Yeah."

"Which could take awhile, especially considering all the communications weirdness."

"Yeah."

"So what do you think? Do we stick to the plan?"

It took Alex a moment to realize Rachel was genuinely asking her opinion on what they should do next.

It took her several moments to realize that they were making a decision that could, in a very real way, affect the entire world.

Alex had never before felt more scared—or more *powerful*.

"We keep going," she said finally. "We go, and we find the sword, and we figure out how to counter all this ancient language business."

"Even though we don't really know what the hell we're doing."

Alex closed her eyes and decided to try and enjoy this new feeling. "Let's think of it as on-the-job training."

* * *

That evening, a bit less than an hour after darkness had fallen, a blanket-covered Alex slumped down in the back seat of the rental car, which was parked across the street and down half a block from the main entrance of the Steinholz Museum. It was not lost on her how similar and yet how completely different this experience was from sitting in the back of an armored van, where she would have been on any other mission at this point. To her surprise, after resenting the vans so bitterly all those years, she now felt exposed and vulnerable in the car.

A slightly fuzzy electronic voice whispered, "Alex. You there?"

Alex reached under the blanket and picked up a very basic, short-range walkie-talkie that Rachel had found in an electronics shop that afternoon. They were betting that whatever mysterious electronic static SKAR was beaming around wouldn't be attuned to something used by a couple of kids playing spy in their backyard.

The bet paid off, it seemed, as they were to be able to use the walkie-talkies with impunity. Alex didn't think it was funny, though, when Rachel pointed out that they more or less *were* a couple of kids playing spy in their backyard.

Alex hit a button on the radio and murmured, "Yeah. Everything okay?"

Inside the museum, which was ten minutes away from closing, Rachel stood in a supply closet in a women's restroom, keeping careful watch for anyone coming in. She whispered into the walkie-talkie, "So far so good. I don't think anybody knows that *we* know about this place at all, so I'm hoping I'll be able to get down into the restricted areas without too much grief. You just keep an eye out for anything that looks like trouble."

"You got it." Her walkie-talkie went silent. Alex continued peering over the edge of the window. The Steinholz Museum primarily featured modern art, and the building itself reflected that, since it was composed mostly of glass and steel. Alex thought it was one of the ugliest buildings she'd ever seen.

A few cars rolled past. Pedestrians ambled along the sidewalks. Everything was quiet.

* * *

Once ten minutes had ticked by, Rachel crept out of the supply closet and risked a look out the restroom door.

The corridor outside was deserted and dim. Only every third light burned. Rachel took a deep breath and moved as quietly as she could toward a stairwell door bearing words in German that translated to "AUTHORIZED PERSONNEL ONLY."

* * *

From Alex's vantage point, the museum did indeed look very quiet. The last of the patrons drifted away, and most of the lights flickered or cut off.

But inside, one floor up from where Rachel had hidden in the restroom, one of the security guards glanced around, stepped into a shadowed alcove, and pulled off the false beard and moustache he'd been wearing. The shirt and hat followed. Then, dressed in utilitarian black clothes, the young man who had called himself David set off down the hallway toward a service elevator, an ugly, black, semiautomatic pistol held comfortably in one hand.

* * *

At that moment, in the museum's lowest level, the grille cover of a ventilation shaft quietly worked loose from its mountings. A delicate hand in a black leather glove pulled the grille back into the shaft, and then a lithe female body wriggled out and dropped silently to the floor. Brushing one stray tendril of blonde hair away from her face, Babette stood, surveyed her surroundings, then pulled a long, thin knife from a sheath strapped to her wrist and headed toward the basement's upstairs exit.

* * *

Outside on the street, Alex's vigil yielded results she'd quite literally never expected. As she watched, a sleek, blood-red sports car pulled up and stopped on the street directly in front of the museum, nowhere near an actual parking space. Alex frowned at the driver's audacity, and then the door opened and the driver stepped out.

Alex's heart didn't just skip a beat. For a moment, she thought it had simply stopped beating for good.

Even from a distance she recognized Sabre Cromwell instantly, his face more handsome than any movie star she could think of, yet at the same time, terrifying. Cromwell glanced around before mounting the marble stairs to the museum's front door, and the confidence he projected was palpable. He believed the world was his for the taking, and his attitude was so overpowering, Alex could do little more than cringe.

She watched, fascinated, as he moved up the stairs with fluid grace, then disappeared inside. Alex had already grabbed the walkie-talkie and was trying to hit the right button with her thumb, but kept missing it. Finally she glanced down, hit the proper button, and took a breath to say, "Rachel!"

Suddenly, the window closest to her feet exploded inward in a shower of glass. A man's hand reached into the car and clamped down on Alex's ankle . . . and the air filled with that horrible, brain-scraping *muttering* that she had first heard at Professor MacMillan's office. Alex got a good look at the man's face through the shattered window: skin like a fish's belly; eyes showing nothing but whites.

The man was a SKAR zombie, just like the ones in Professor MacMillan's office.

Alex shrieked and dropped the radio, kicking and scrambling away. She bashed the zombie's hand hard enough to make him lose his grip on her leg. In response he shoved his whole upper body into the car.

Again, Alex shrieked. She fumbled with the door latch, then her cry rose sharply as another zombie pressed his face against the glass just inches from her. He balled up his fist and struck the window, but it didn't break. As he drew back for another try, Alex looked wildly around and saw two more zombies out the back window, then one leaning over the windshield.

She was surrounded.

The glass right next to her shattered as the second zombie's fist came through it.

chapter nineteen

Keeping to the shadows as much as possible, Rachel crept forward, moving down a long, dimly lit hallway.

She'd already snuck past two security guards, but neither of them had seemed particularly threatening. She began to get the idea that most of the museum's staff were just regular, ordinary working people, and that any involvement SKAR had must be restricted to those basement levels.

Or, she considered with a sinking feeling in her gut, maybe there wasn't any SKAR involvement here at all.

Maybe she was wrong about this place. Maybe the fact that one of those zombie guys worked here was the sheerest of coincidences.

Wrong or not, she kept looking for another flight of stairs. Slowly, quietly, she opened a door.

Rachel now found herself in an underground grid of corridors that led to what looked like laboratories. The place was all white paint and metal doors and looked more like a hospital than a museum.

Still, though, she'd run across no actual personnel. The creeping doubt began to nag at her again, more persistent this time . . . and then she saw them. Two people, a man and a woman dressed in white lab coats, came out of one doorway and headed toward another at the end of the hall. Immediately, Rachel's hackles were raised.

She hadn't spent the last five years as a firefighter without talking to plenty of cops and former cops. Their hunches and gut feelings—based on experience, as well as subconscious analysis of clues such as facial expressions and body language—had rubbed off on her enough to know that this pair should be filed under "Suspicious" with a capital "S."

Drawing in a deep breath, Rachel decided to go with the straightforward approach.

"Hey, I'm glad I caught you guys," she called out in German, brazenly walking up to them.

The pair turned and looked at her blankly. Not the blankness of zombification; they simply didn't recognize her.

"I'm sorry, miss, but you can't be down here," the man answered, also in German. "There's no exit this way. You'll have to go back up and find a security guard to let you out of the museum."

"Thanks, that's very helpful," Rachel said, and swung one extended arm like a baseball bat, the edge of her hand connecting with his mandibular joint—the place many fighters referred to as "the button."

It worked. The man switched off, slumping to the floor like the proverbial marionette with cut strings.

The woman opened her mouth to scream, but Rachel sprang forward, locking her arms around the woman's throat in a vicious chokehold. She knew that just a tiny bit of extra pressure would cut off both the oxygen to the woman's lungs and the blood supply to her brain. Whispering, Rachel said, "You're going to take me inside now."

The woman tried to nod. That was good enough. Still in Rachel's chokehold, she opened a panel beside the door she'd been about to enter and punched a seven-digit code into a keypad.

The door slid readily open, and Rachel steered the woman inside.

A long hallway greeted them; the antiseptic smell grew stronger. Maybe sixty feet ahead of them was a large set of double doors on the right. The doors had a broad, red stripe painted across them.

"I'm going to ask you two questions, and I don't want any nonsense," Rachel whispered. The woman blinked rapidly and nodded as much as she was able. "First question: is the Vosarak Sword down there?" More nods. Rachel exhaled a long, slow breath. Then, "Is it guarded?"

An emphatic nod.

Rachel closed her eyes for a moment. Then she opened them, applied the necessary pressure, and put the woman to sleep. Checking her pulse to make sure she was okay, Rachel dragged her into an empty room nearby, gagged her with a strip torn off of the lab coat, then bound her with the cords from a couple of floor lamps close by.

Exiting the room, Rachel turned right and approached the red-striped double doors, then pushed one open and went through it.

* * *

Outside, back in the rental car, Alex slid down onto her back and kicked violently upward at the moonroof with both feet.

It didn't budge.

She cried out in fear and frustration, and kicked again. This time the glass gave a tiny bit. Fighting off grasping hands, trying her best to keep the doors locked, Alex let out a huge grunt of effort and kicked as hard as she could.

The moonroof popped out of the car's body and slid down the windshield. One of the zombies noticed this and had just started to make noises about it, when Alex shot up out of the newly created opening quick as a rabbit, adrenaline practically gushing through her.

Terrified and beyond panicked, she crouched on the roof of the car for a moment, gazing wildly around her at the bizarre mind-damaged goons trying to grab her. Then she shrieked again and leaped off the car's roof, right over one of the zombies' heads. She landed hard, but got to her feet and sprinted straight toward the darkened museum.

* * *

Seconds earlier, when Rachel pushed through the red-striped double doors in the bare, spartan hallway, she understood in a flash why getting this far had been so easy: all of the security was down here. She slowly raised her hands above her head as twenty commandos in body armor, all of them holding automatic weapons, turned and took aim at her.

The room was little more than a rectangular box and could have been used for any purpose. But the far end of it had been turned into a high-tech, electronically shielded vault—and behind a screen of reinforced bulletproof glass and a crisscrossing web of brilliant green security lasers, mounted on a metal display stand, was the Vosarak Sword.

The commandos seemed to have been in the process of relocating the sword. A heavy wooden crate with an oblong metal case inside lay open nearby, resting on a trolley for easy transport.

The closest of the commandos took a step toward Rachel and spoke in German. "Who are you? Where are Billings and Screed?"

Rachel glanced out of the corner of her eye at the door behind her. She had heard it latch shut when she came in, and she held grave doubts as to whether she could get it open and make it through before being shot full of holes.

"You mean the man and the woman in white coats?"

The commando raised an eyebrow.

"They, uh . . . they said I could use the restroom down here? I *really* have to go."

The commando snorted, turned his head to give an order, and at that moment the door opened behind Rachel and a small, round object flew into the room and bounced on the floor in the midst of the armed men. From the door, so low that only she could hear it, Rachel caught a terse whisper: "*Close your eyes.*"

She did, and later she would wonder what it must have been like to experience this with open eyes, because even with hers squeezed shut, the room got so bright everything became a blue-green glare.

Rachel felt something brush past her, and after blinking a few times, she could make out a lean, handsome, young Asian man. He looked oddly familiar to her; he was in the process of beating the living hell out of the stunned, dazed commandos with his bare hands.

"You're that guy," she said, as the last of the commandos slumped over onto the floor.

The young man had fought like a demon. He had torn through the mercenaries as if they'd been standing still. Whether they'd been blinded or not, that was quite a feat.

"David. You were talking to Alex."

"I'm someone who doesn't have time to explain himself," David said. His voice held no trace of a French accent. Rather his words came out in perfect, non-regional American English. Without looking at Rachel, he went immediately to a control panel situated close to the glass vault behind which the sword stood. "Just stay out of my way for a couple of minutes, all right?"

"Pardon me, miss," said a very pleasant, feminine voice, again from right behind Rachel.

Rachel stiffened. She recognized that voice, just as she felt the point of a knife graze her throat.

David whipped his head around and his eyes narrowed. Impatiently, he said, "Yvette, for the love of God."

"Move away from that control panel, David," the woman said.

Before David could respond, Rachel spoke to Babette-Yvette-whatever-the-hell-her-name-was. "I haven't met too many people from Luxembourg before."

The woman took a step forward to look into Rachel's face, openly surprised. The knife didn't move, but Rachel smiled at the woman's obvious shock.

"I'm good with accents," Rachel said a little smugly.

David hadn't moved away from the control panel.

"Yes, well . . ." The knife still in one hand, the woman pulled a tiny Derringer pistol from her pocket and backed away from Rachel, aiming the diminutive gun at her chest. "You and your accents stay right where you are. I shan't be long."

David had his gun in his hand as well, though he pointed it at the floor. "You're crazy if you think I'm going to let you take this, Yvette."

"My country can do just as much with it as South Korea can. Step aside. You know I can get through the encryption ten times faster than you." She produced a small electronic device from one pocket.

David's face darkened. "*That's* your big advantage? A decoder? I've got one of those mysel—"

Rachel had moved away from the doors, closer to one corner of the room, where she could see both David and the woman named Yvette. But a flash of movement caught her eye, and she turned to see the door open a third time . . . as Sabre Cromwell sauntered through it.

His voice flowed out smoothly, rich with Australian intonations. "Why don't the *both* of you step aside, so I don't have to kill you here on the spot?"

Rachel stared. In person, Cromwell's charisma was overpowering; he reminded her of a wickedly beautiful, perfectly crafted blade: finely wrought enough to be a work of art, but undeniably created for killing.

David gritted out, "*Cromwell . . .*"

Yvette slowly, reluctantly lowered her gun. Cromwell didn't even appear to be armed, and had made no physically threatening move. Yet she *still* lowered her weapon.

Near where Rachel stood, one of the commandos groaned, opened his eyes, and sat up.

"Rouse the rest of your boys, Lieutenant," Cromwell said to the commando. "We're having ourselves a little clambake."

* * *

On the street, Alex wasn't sure her feet even touched the ground on every step, she ran so fast. Risking a quick glance over her shoulder, she saw the zombies coming after her, and again, they were *nothing* like what she'd seen in the movies the BGO had piped into the dorms on weekends. She couldn't tell if they were actually gaining on her, but she thought they might be, and she had no intention of taking any chances.

Then she glanced up and saw the massive glass doors at the top of the stairs. She was sure they'd be locked, but she was also sure she had to get inside no matter what. Heavy-looking concrete planters lined the front stairs, so Alex grabbed one. For a second, she thought it would wrench her arms out of their sockets with its weight . . . but she heaved it straight through the right-hand door. Well, more like half heaved, half dropped—or maybe just sort of shoved. But in any case, it did the job; the door shattered into thousands of pieces, and Alex ducked through the doorway, jumped over the planter, and dashed into the museum.

Three things flashed over the surface of her mind, little skittering side thoughts.

The first was that if the SKAR zombies were here, then SKAR probably knew she and Rachel were here, and Rachel was in an insane amount of danger.

Second, by breaking the window, she'd no doubt set off all kinds of alarms and would be drawing heavy attention to herself.

The third thing was *Bring on the attention!* She didn't think SKAR really wanted the regular German police force made aware of their presence or their activities.

Unless SKAR already owned the German police force . . .

Never mind that! Rachel had been heading downstairs. Alex looked for an elevator or a stairwell, and almost ran nose-first into a regular museum security guard, who seemed as surprised to see her as she was to see him.

The guard asked some kind of outraged question in German and waved at the shattered glass all over the lobby floor. Alex raced past him. "Sorry! Stairs! Need! Aaah!"

A couple of seconds later she heard the guard scream. *Damn. Here come the zombies.*

There! An elevator!

"Let it be here, let it be here," she whispered, punching the button with the arrow pointed downward. A bell dinged and the doors slid open. With a slightly louder, "Thank you!" she dashed inside and hit the "doors close" button.

As the doors slid shut, she saw the first of the zombies come around a corner. There was no question that he spotted her in the elevator.

The number selection in the car went from five at the top to one at the bottom, then—*yes!*—there was one button below the others. She stabbed it and felt the elevator lurch into motion.

Twenty seconds later, the elevator came to a stop, the doors opened again, and at that instant a terrible crash came from directly above her head. Waxy hands wrenched the roof access panel open. Alex looked up into the faces of two of the zombies.

Two more crashes immediately followed as more of them dropped down the shaft onto the roof of the elevator.

Alex screamed, "Rachel!" at the top of her lungs and dashed out of the elevator into a very dimly lit, bare white hallway. The only light she could see spilled out from a nearby set of double doors painted with a broad red stripe. She sprinted straight for it, calling out Rachel's name again.

One of the double doors opened half a second before she got there. A tall man in what she thought was body armor peered out into the hallway, obviously confused, but Alex didn't wait to hear anything he might have said. *Would've been in German anyway*, she thought, and dashed past him into the room.

A bizarre spectacle greeted her. Around the walls, more men in body armor looked as if they were struggling to stand up, like they'd all been knocked down by an earthquake or something. At the room's far end, behind some kind of barrier that looked like it came out of a science fiction movie, was the Vosarak Sword—but she couldn't get excited about that, because in the middle of the room stood Rachel, David, and David's homicidal-spy girlfriend.

Alex felt a thudding sensation in her stomach at the sight of David. Sort of a one-two punch, as she was first caught completely off-guard by seeing him here, and then because that single glance told her that he hadn't been even remotely honest with her before. Grad students don't show up in places like this, dressed all in black, holding guns and standing in front of priceless artifacts.

Then a third blow, more painful than the first two: *Why didn't I see this before? God, I'm so stupid!* David and the blonde were working together. They *had* to be. *They set me up!*

Alex started to say something to him, and then her voice shriveled and died as she skidded to a dead stop right in front of Sabre Cromwell. He grinned down at her with delighted recognition. "*You*," Cromwell said.

And he might have said more, but he didn't get the chance. The five SKAR zombies came barreling into the room and crashed straight into him and Alex, sending them to the floor in a huge chaotic tangle.

chapter twenty

At that point, an awful lot of things happened at once.

Alex's recollection of it later was on the hazy side, like seeing a film out of focus, with only a few frames that clicked into clarity. But it was a film with the soundtrack cranked all the way up: screams, gunfire, more screams.

A black-booted foot snapped out and kicked Alex in the thigh, and her own screams added to the cacophony. Then a hand clamped down on her wrist and dragged her across the floor, through the chaos of limbs, and she thought she'd go deaf from the thunderous noise.

One frame, frozen in Alex's head: the crazy blonde woman David had called Babette, her hands striking like vipers into the throng.

Another: David and Sabre Cromwell fighting like blurs amid the commandos and the SKAR zombies.

A third: Rachel scooping up a small electronic device that had fallen to the floor.

It all happened so fast.

There was a gap, then, and Alex wondered if she got hit on the head, since the next few minutes dissolved into a harsh green smear.

And then the hand grabbed her wrist again, and she and Rachel burst out through the double doors and ran for the elevator. Rachel ignored it and hit the staircase just beyond it, yanking Alex up behind her, up and up the stairs that never seemed to end, and not until they emerged into the main lobby and dashed toward the shattered doors did Alex realize: Rachel had the Vosarak Sword in her other hand!

Whether from physical exhaustion, or maybe emotional exhaustion, or possibly blunt head trauma, Alex's lips widened into a huge grin. She started to speak, but Rachel said, "Grin later! Run now!"

Alex obligingly moved her feet.

They'd done it. They had the sword!

Now it was just a matter of *keeping* it.

* * *

Half an hour later, Alex stood in a tiny public bathroom attached to an automobile service station that didn't look as if it got much traffic. A couple of large bags from a department store sat near her feet, and just beyond them a guitar case leaned against the wall. It wasn't easy, finding a case the Vosarak Sword would fit into, but they did it.

Quietly, Alex said, "Wow . . . I wouldn't have thought it would make that big a difference."

She watched Rachel, who stood in front of the restroom's one sink, applying a substance to her hair which was both straightening it and turning it jet black. Of course, it also made the hair look really greasy, but to Alex's utter lack of surprise, Rachel looked good that way. Plus the change to her hair completely altered Rachel's appearance. Now that she'd changed clothes and done this, one pair of dark glasses later and she'd be almost unrecognizable.

"Yeah," Rachel answered, distracted. "I did this for Halloween one year . . . works for some people, doesn't for others." She washed her hands, then turned to face Alex. "Okay, your turn."

Alex couldn't help but be a little excited. Yes, the circumstances were beyond lousy, but the thought of having Rachel give her a makeover of *any* kind, even one born out of desperation, was pretty appealing. "What are you going to do? Color my hair, too? You're not going to cut it off, are you?"

Without answering, Rachel picked up one of the bags, then half leaned, half sat back against the edge of the sink. Alex shot her a quizzical look. "Something wrong?"

"I think . . ." Rachel started, uneasy. "I think you're probably not going to like this, but I also think it's the best course of action. This will really throw them off our trail if we do it right."

"What're you talking about?"

Rachel reached into the bag and pulled out a pair of jeans, a shirt, and an American baseball cap. There were no hair products at all. It hit Alex hard what Rachel was about to ask her to do. "You want me to dress like a *guy*."

"I'm sorry. But they're looking for two females, and a female traveling with a boy might just slip right past them."

Frowning, Alex took the shirt and jeans from Rachel and eyed them critically. "There's nothing, I mean, I don't see anything, y'know, *overtly* masculine about this stuff."

"Well . . ." Rachel grew even more uncomfortable. "If we push all your hair under the cap, and put the ponytail down inside your shirt, then flip the collar up . . ."

Alex sagged. "Right. Right. Take away the long hair, make sure I'm not wearing any makeup at all, dress in clothes that don't *have* to be masculine. Just as long as they're not *feminine*, and . . ."

She didn't want to say the rest of the words out loud. *From the neck down I can pass as a boy, no problem.*

"I've got a map of the subway routes," Rachel said, obviously desperate to change the subject. "The end of one line stops about an eighth of a mile from the rendezvous point. We should get you dressed and get going, since we don't know *when* we're supposed to meet our guys, only *where*."

Alex sighed and said, "Yeah, yeah, I know," then set the shirt and jeans on the sink and slipped off her shoes.

* * *

Everything was quiet as Alex and Rachel made their way toward the subway station. No one gave a second glance to the now black-haired Rachel with her guitar case, and no one looked at Alex at all. Apparently, she was even more unremarkable as a boy.

Strangely enough, this didn't bother her. She had expected it would, and for a few minutes she sat on a huge pile of righteous indignation over the whole situation. But then it occurred to her: this is what spies do. And like it or not, right now she and Rachel were spies. Operating in a foreign country under false identities, working to gain something that would benefit their own nation? Sure, it would benefit the rest of the world, too, but still.

And spies needed to be unobtrusive. Inconspicuous.

Plain.

I could be good at this, she thought, and grinned a little.

"Okay, here we go," Rachel said as they entered the station. A huge map hung on a wall nearby, and she glanced at it to verify their route. "We need to head for Platform 7."

More people crowded the subway than Alex had expected, and Platform 7 was particularly densely packed. Still, they made their way through the crowd toward the bright yellow train. Everything was normal. Rachel looked over her shoulder and said, "Hey, we need to hurry. It's about to leave."

She was right. People jammed aboard the train, ducking on at the last minute. Alex stuck close to Rachel, right behind her, and as Rachel followed the rest of the passengers and got on board . . . a huge, fat man pulling his short, fat son bulled past her, shoving her out of the way to get on the train.

Alex stumbled. The man had to weigh four times what she did. But she righted herself and was about to try to slip past him when an equally fat woman, no doubt the wife and mother, bustled up and bumped Alex back again.

The fat woman had just squeezed in when the doors slid shut.

Alex leaped forward and pulled at the doors, but she might as well have been pulling at stone. She looked in through the glass and saw Rachel, who had just realized Alex wasn't on the train with her.

Alex couldn't tell which of them this distressed more.

Immediately, Rachel pulled out her walkie-talkie, and Alex did the same, just as the train began to move.

The radio squawked: "Alex!"

"I couldn't get on! What do I do?"

"Okay, okay, you know where the rendezvous point is, right?"

"Yeah. Yeah, you showed me on the map."

"Then meet me there! Take the next train! It's supposed to be here in five minutes—if you get on the very next train we shouldn't get more than half a mile apart."

"Okay . . . okay, yeah, I'll do it."

"Stay safe," Rachel said.

Alex responded, "All right," in a very small voice.

She let the hand holding the radio drop to her side, then stood there, alone in the middle of the crowd, feeling incredibly stupid.

chapter twenty-one

"This is okay," Alex whispered. The sound of her own voice wasn't as comforting as she would have liked. "I'm going to wait for the next train, get on the train, go to the place, and everything will be fine."

The platform began to fill up again. Not as tightly packed as it had been, but there were quite a few people around her. Alex stuck her hands in her pockets and turned in a circle, glancing casually from person to person, and for a moment or two the reality of her situation struck her as both amazing and absurd.

Only a couple of days before, her whole experience with the world had consisted of four things: the insides of armored vans, the insides of the Square, the insides of her new condo, and the stuff she saw on television.

Now she was standing in a subway station in Germany, pursued by who knew how many fascist nutjobs, completely cut off from the BGO, while she tried to complete a secret mission that revolved around a *sword*, for crying out loud. It was ridiculous! She felt sort of *detached* . . . as if she were waiting for a commercial break in her own life.

This reverie came to an abrupt end when a middle-aged man moved away from one of the platform's huge concrete support columns, revealing a woman in a long, dove-gray trench coat standing in the column's shadow.

The woman glided forward, just far enough to reveal her features, and smiled at Alex—whose stomach clenched.

She recognized the woman instantly. The impossibly black hair; the face like a cold, haughty goddess; the pinup girl figure that even a trench coat couldn't completely conceal. Sonnet Ivandrova moved farther out into the light, still smiling, and began to speak . . . in Vosarak.

The words echoed unnaturally around the platform, as if Sonnet were talking into a gigantic bell. Alex stiffened, as did everyone else around her, all of them hearing the words, none of them realizing what it was.

Desperately hoping she wouldn't screw it up, Alex chattered off the phrase Rachel had drilled into her on the road trip from Paris.

Sonnet Ivandrova's voice seemed to change in timbre. The bell-like tones abruptly went flat and muffled, as if a thick goosedown pillow had been shoved into the bell. Sonnet frowned and spoke louder, her brows drawing together; she looked like one of the Furies, but Alex didn't let up. She kept repeating the phrase until Sonnet broke off her chanting.

But then Sonnet's smile came back as everyone else on the platform turned to face Alex, their skin draining of color and their eyes gyrating crazily in their heads.

As soon as she saw the first pair of all-white, unseeing eyes, Alex dropped her bags, spun on her heel, and sprinted back toward the stairs that led up to the street. Hand after hand grabbed at her, tried to stop her, but she twisted and made it to the stairs unharmed.

Two at a time, she climbed them, practically jumping each time, and flashed out onto the pedestrian-heavy sidewalk at full speed. Heavy, thumping footsteps echoed up out of the stairway behind her, but she *had* to take a second to get her bearings.

The train was going . . . Alex glanced down a busy street. *That way.* She took off running again.

A couple of frantic glances behind her let her know she'd outdistanced the grotesque Insta-Zombies. But her walkie-talkie was back there on the subway platform, and with no way to contact Rachel, she was in serious trouble and knew it.

She triggered the proximity sensor masquerading as a wristwatch. Rachel was stationary, but she was also already more than a quarter mile away. Much farther and the sensor would start to flash red . . . and then Rachel would vanish in a sparkling shower of tiny lights, leaving the Vosarak Sword in its guitar case just lying there, unprotected, waiting for any agent of SKAR to come along and pick it up.

Alex's breath began to burn with every inhalation and exhalation, and already her feet and knees were complaining. A realization began to set in: *I'm not going to make it.*

She'd failed. Failed in the first mission where she ever did anything besides sit on her butt. There was *no way* she could catch a subway train on foot, no matter how many stops it had to make. She might as well just quit, sit down right here, and wait for Sonnet Ivandrova or Sabre Cromwell or even the Gray Baron himself to drive up, knock her over the head, and stuff her in a sack.

God, wouldn't that be so much easier than this? She might as well try to outrace a 747 on a bicycle.

But her feet didn't stop. She didn't slow down.

Even though it hurt, she kept on . . . and as Alex scowled and curled her lips back, she ran *faster.*

Screw failure. Screw giving up. I have a job to do, don't I? Right now no one else on the planet could do what needed to be done. And she'd be *damned* if it didn't get done because she just sat down and refused to try.

Alex ran and ran—one block, two blocks, then four, then seven. It felt as if her feet were going to break and fall off, but she kept going. Her heart, she was pretty sure, was about to burst like a water balloon. But she kept going. And just when her vision actually began to get a little bit dark around the edges . . . she saw a car out of the corner of her eye veer sharply toward her, saw a door fly open, and then slender but surprisingly strong arms grabbed her and dragged her into the back seat. The door thumped against her thigh as it closed, and she stared madly around her, gasping for breath.

Babette gave her an incongruously friendly smile. She sat right next to Alex on the back seat. "Look at you," she said, still smiling. "You're just like Franka Potente in *Run Lola Run*."

Alex continued gasping, trying desperately to get her breath back. Babette said to the driver, "Did you ever see that film, David? It's quite good. A bit *avant garde*, but it *is* German, after all."

David glanced quickly at the back seat before returning his eyes to the road. When he spoke, his voice held no trace of the French accent Alex had found so charming; this time he could have been from Nebraska. "I'm afraid I missed that one." He winked at Alex in the rearview mirror. "You okay? What's going on?"

Alex wheezed and gasped. "Don't . . . don't *wink* at me . . . you son of a *bitch*."

Her anger seemed to catch both of them off guard. David's eyes got huge. "Huh? What'd *I* do?"

Alex punched the back of the seat before her. "You set me up! 'Oh, there's my ex, let's go take a walk, I'll just lure you away so she can bash you over the head.' Too bad it didn't work out, *Dah-veed*."

David's eyes stayed huge, but his astonishment turned (to Alex's extreme annoyance) to amusement. "Oh, Alex, you're *way* off base."

He sounded convincing. Alarmingly so, in fact. Alex looked from him to Babette and back, and saw that they both seemed to find her accusation pretty funny. "You weren't working together?"

"Not then," Babette said, still very friendly. "Not usually, for that matter. Sweetheart, I stole you right out from under David's nose. You should have seen his face!"

"Just for the record," David said, sounding a little defensive, "all that tie-you-to-the-chair stuff is *completely* not my style. I was just going to talk you out of some intel."

Babette made a sound like "feh."

Alex didn't think she could have been any more confused. "Who *are* you people?"

Babette chuckled. "I suppose we owe you that much. Besides, it's not as if we exist on any official records anywhere." She held out one hand politely. "My name is Yvette LeChance."

Alex shook the hand, bewildered. Yvette's personality had undergone as radical a transformation as any she'd ever seen, from the cold bitch who tried to drug her in the back of a florist shop to the refined young woman sitting next to her now.

"My name really *is* David," the driver said. "David Yu. I'm South Korean. And Yvette is from Luxembourg; she's just too embarrassed to admit it."

Yvette popped David in the back of the head. *Playfully.* Maybe they didn't always work together, but the two of them obviously knew each other, had *known* each other for some time.

"So why were you running?" Yvette asked. "Is there somewhere you need to be?"

The question stopped Alex cold. *This* was the source of help she so desperately needed? Two people that she had every reason *not* to trust?

Yvette seemed to read the caution in Alex's face. "Look, here's where we are. David and I both want the Vosarak Sword, we each want to take it back home, but we've gotten a pretty good idea that if we don't get it back at all, each of our countries will suffer." Then a fraction less certain, she said, "It's starting to look like the whole planet might suffer."

Alex thought furiously. She knew she shouldn't let go of any more information than necessary, but—she checked her sensor—thank God they were going in the right direction. There was only one thing to do.

"Listen, I have *got* to get to the Kohler Air Field. It's a little private place right at the city limits. My, uh, my ride sort of left me; that's why I was running."

David said, "I know the place."

Yvette's eyebrows raised thoughtfully. "Okay. So if we take you there . . . ?"

If they took her there, what?

She didn't have an answer of any kind, really, so to stall for time she checked the proximity sensor again. They were about as close to Rachel as when she had checked it the last time, meaning Rachel was still on the move.

Alex decided to bluff it. "You take me there, and I'll tell you everything you ever wanted to know. And believe me, I know plenty. But you're a hundred percent correct about the whole world getting shafted if we don't get the sword back. So please, if you know this place, get me there as fast as you can."

chapter twenty-two

The next fifteen minutes were spent in a kind of slow, agonized torture, even as David whipped the car through the thick metropolitan traffic. If not for each of the stops the subway train made, there was no way Alex could have stayed within the half-mile safety limit. She could only imagine what Rachel must be thinking, watching the uncomfortable number display on her own sensor.

Yvette LeChance tried to lighten Alex's mood with conversation. "You're quite the mystery to us, you know," she said pleasantly. "You show up hip-deep in a situation that maybe fifty people in the world know about, and yet you don't appear to have *anything* in the way of formal training. Plus, and I mean no offense by this, are you even of legal age?"

David spoke up, a slightly protective edge to his voice. "There's no need to harass her, Yvette."

Alex felt a sudden urge to lean over the seat and kiss David on the cheek.

"My apologies," Yvette went on blithely. "But still, I think the line of questioning is reasonable. Care to enlighten us?"

Alex narrowed her eyes at Yvette in what she hoped was a clever mask for how fast her mind was racing. "I don't think you have any room to talk about deceiving appearances," she said after a moment. "What are you, twenty? Twenty-one? Shouldn't you still be in college?"

"Zing," David said.

Alex couldn't resist. "You're not any better, 'David.' How come you sounded like a French guy to begin with, and now you're talking like an American sportscaster?"

He glanced over the seat again. "I was born in Seoul, but I went to school in Cincinnati." Eyes back on the road, he said, "I like to think it's given me an appreciation for the best that both Korean and American girls have to offer."

Alex blushed deeply at that, which Yvette seemed to find immensely entertaining.

"David, you silver-tongued devil!" she exclaimed. "You've charmed young Alex right to the bone."

"I think you're both insane," Alex said sullenly. "*You're* government operatives? For real? How is that even possible? I mean, I said it before, but it's true—you're both so *young*."

"Ah, little girl," Yvette said with an infuriating mix of condescension and big-sisterly understanding, "there is so much you do not know, so many things you have not seen."

Alex glared at her, thinking, *Tell me something I don't know.*

Then David shouted, "Look out!" and swerved the car sharply to the right. Yvette grabbed Alex's head and forced it down almost to the floorboard just before the glass of the back window, the driver's rearview mirror, and the front passenger window exploded. Only a second later did it register on Alex's mind that she'd heard the gunfire, *crack crack crack*, as three bullets tore through the car.

Alex risked a peek outside as David fought to keep the car on the street. She saw a long, low, black sedan swerving and fighting through traffic beside them. One window was open, and a burly man in a black suit leaned out of it, firing a gigantic handgun at them.

"Get your head down, damn it!" Yvette screamed, and Alex did what she was told, ducking back below sight level.

Yvette produced a pistol of her own. Popping up like a target in a shooting gallery, she squeezed off somewhere between three and five rounds so fast that Alex couldn't keep track of them. She thought she heard a man's voice cry out in pain, then Yvette dropped back down as the black sedan slammed into them again.

David struggled with the wheel, just barely able to keep the car on the road. He shouted in surprise. Even from where she was, Alex could see that the black sedan had stayed very close to them, almost touching, and that another man was actually climbing out of the open window, snarling at their car.

It was Sabre Cromwell.

Yvette saw him at the same time as Alex did, and said, "Oh shit."

David swerved away from the sedan and shouted, "Switch places with me!"

Certain she hadn't just heard that, Alex said, *"Switch places?"* but Yvette was already moving. She clambered into the front seat as David slithered backward and dropped down beside Alex. Yvette slid in behind the wheel and seamlessly took over.

But the craziness had just begun. The black sedan came back, and Alex saw Sabre Cromwell perched on its roof. When it got within six feet of them, Cromwell leaped off, and his impact made a heavy *thud* on their own roof.

Without a word, David climbed through the shattered back window, staring at Cromwell with scary determination.

Just then, the car passed a building with a long picture window, and she saw David and Cromwell actually fighting on the roof of the car, struggling and striking and somehow managing to avoid being flung violently off.

"You've got to stop!" she shouted to Yvette. "You're going to get David killed!"

"Nonsense. It'll take more than a little car crash to kill him."

Alex wasn't sure what she meant, but before she could ask, a second black sedan came zooming toward them on the opposite side from the first one.

"Little detour," Yvette said, still with her white-knuckled grip on the wheel and her tightly clenched jaw. She swerved the car onto a side street (Alex heard the *thump* as David and Cromwell both hit the roof, but didn't see anyone roll off the car) and sped into an outdoor bazaar filled with vendor's stalls and huge displays of products ranging from food to stuffed animals.

"What are you *doing?*" Alex yelled, but Yvette didn't answer. She threaded the car nimbly down the center aisle, lying on the horn to force people out of the way, and Alex saw the wisdom of her action: there was no room for the sedans to follow unless they fell in behind her.

The flaw in Yvette's plan became obvious when the two black cars simply bulldozed through the stalls and displays, smashing and trashing fruit, with alligator-skin wallets and teddy bears flying left and right.

Alex stared back at the pursuers. "We're not losing them!"

"I can *see* that," Yvette said tersely. "If I can just get past thi—" but her words cut off as the car hit an unseen obstruction and lofted completely into the air, spinning on its axis like a bullet fired from a gun.

The world slowed down for Alex just then.

Her brain tried to make sense of what was going on, throwing out a list of comparisons. At first it was, *Oh, okay, this is like a roller coaster in a corkscrew spin,* but then the sensations immediately intensified, and then she thought, *Better make that a centrifuge, where the floor falls away and you're stuck to the wall,* and all the while the fear and terror were building up in her gut and she realized she was in serious danger of vomiting explosively—the churning, spinning, crushing torture was replaced with cool air on her face, and the spinning was gone, but she had no idea what was happening and realized she'd squeezed her eyes shut, and when she opened them, reality threatened to stop her heart.

She'd been thrown from the car.

The violent forces of the spinning vehicle had ejected her through some open window somewhere, and then the only thing she saw she didn't recognize: a mass of something green and fuzzy. When the impact came, it was so brutal that she felt as if the Earth had grown a gigantic fist and hammered her whole body with it.

chapter twenty-three

Kohler Air Field was a relatively tiny, privately owned place just inside the city limits. Mainly used for high-level corporate aircraft and charter flights, it had just a single runway with a hangar and office at one end. On the other side of the hangar were two small helipads. The helipads stood empty, and only one airplane—a small twin-engine private jet—was parked near the hangar at the head of the runway.

Rachel walked warily across the tarmac toward the office, carrying the guitar case close. She felt very exposed. The place seemed deserted, which was good, since she didn't feel like answering anybody's questions. Getting here on foot from the train station had proven to be slow and awkward, though, and the longer she walked, the less she liked the whole situation.

Not to mention Alex. Their separation opened up a whole other world of anxiety that Rachel chose not to think about at the moment. She checked her proximity sensor. According to the readout, Alex was still within the safety range, but not getting any closer.

She reached the edge of the parking lot and made her way toward the office. She could hear faint traffic noises in the distance, and a plane flew far overhead, leaving a slow white trail across the sky. But as far as the airfield went, she might as well have been the last woman on Earth.

* * *

Time passed.

How long . . . ?

When Alex began to regain consciousness, her first thought was, *Quit making all that noise!* Then she realized the noise was her own ears ringing, a discovery soon followed by a wide variety of aches throughout the rest of her body. She was pretty sure that every inch of her, from toenails to eyelashes, was in pain.

Alex lay sprawled in the middle of a ruined display of some kind of fuzzy green fruit she didn't recognize. *I guess even fruit hurts if you hit it hard enough,* she thought, getting slowly to her feet. *Oh, God, I'm all sticky, too! How disgusting.* She patted herself down, carefully moved all of her joints—and gasped when she tried to flex her left wrist.

Alex had never had any broken bones before, so she had no frame of reference as to how they felt. But she was pretty sure her wrist was fractured. As she watched, she thought she could see it swelling, and the pain throbbed with every heartbeat.

Then a thought struck her, and she carefully, gingerly turned the proximity sensor around from where it had gotten skewed on her arm. It still worked, the readout flashing the same as always.

Thing's tougher than I am, she thought with a sense of relief that surprised her. A broken wrist was one thing, but if that sensor had been damaged . . . she didn't want to consider it.

Glancing around, she saw several German citizens poking their heads out of the various hiding places where they had dived when the cars crashed. She spotted one of the black cars; it was upside down, maybe forty feet away. When she looked farther up the street, she thought she saw part of the other car underneath a transfer truck that was parked in front of a grocery store.

She couldn't see David and Yvette's car anywhere. No sign of either of them, nor of Sabre Cromwell.

A young woman approached her hesitantly and spoke a few inquisitive words. Alex had no idea what they were, of course, but the woman's tone was along the lines of, "Are you all right?"

She looked down at herself, dressed in boy's clothes and covered in fuzzy green fruit juice . . . Her wrist throbbed again. Suddenly, the numbers she had seen on the sensor's readout finally registered.

Startling the German woman, Alex spun around and looked behind her, then took off at a pained, awkward run, her muscles aching and her wrist getting worse.

It only took her a few seconds to scoot down the alley beside the nearest building. Then she saw a sight beyond hope.

There in front of her stood a large sign written in German. She couldn't tell exactly what the words said, but that didn't matter. What mattered was the biggest one: KOHLER.

Beyond the sign, on the other side of a chain-link fence and a wide expanse of flat, grassy land, was a small runway and a hangar.

Alex hobbled toward the fence, flooded with a sense of relief so strong she half expected it to buoy her up and float her right over the chain links.

chapter twenty-four

Alex's sense of relief didn't fade, but neither did it help her clamber over the fence with a broken wrist. She thought about walking around the fence's perimeter until she came to a gate, but she had no way of knowing where a gate would be or how long that would take. Besides, it was already getting late, the sun had begun to set, and she *really* didn't want to wander around in the dark. Since there didn't seem to be anyone around to question her—the public's attention was focused on the fruit vendor carnage one street over, and she could finally hear sirens approaching—Alex gritted her teeth and set about climbing the fence.

Rachel needs me. I can't wimp out now. I'm not going to be my own sidekick anymore! I'll be my own hero if it kills me.

She had no idea it would be so difficult. With two good hands maybe it wouldn't have been such a nightmare, but with her left hand useless and her wrist hurting worse than ever, it was literally all she could do just to inch her way up. The skin on her right hand tore and bled, and she ripped both her shirt and her jeans, badly scratching the skin underneath.

Finally, what seemed like hours after she started, Alex tipped over the top of the fence and fell to the ground in a heap on the other side. She just lay there for a minute, panting, hoping she hadn't broken anything else. Then she checked the sensor.

According to the tiny device, Rachel was only a couple hundred yards away, apparently on the other side of the hangar, where the helicopters would land. Alex hauled herself up to her feet and set off across the grass at the fastest walk she could manage. Nothing moved around her. She thought the airfield must have been shut down.

Finally, after what seemed like an absurdly long time, Alex reached the edge of the pavement and checked the sensor again. This close to its partner, the sensor's directional indicator was a lot more precise than usual. Rachel wasn't in the waiting room. Alex moved her arm, and watched the LED indicator swing slightly. *Ah-ha.* There was a big stack of crates just inside the hangar on the other side, and the indicator pointed right at it. *Maybe Rachel is crouched down among them?*

Alex quickened her pace. The sooner she rejoined Rachel the better. That thought itself made her smile a little, despite her anxiety and the agony in her wrist. *Never thought I'd be this happy to see an Alex Prime.* She hurried across an expanse of runway and entered the hangar's shadow.

Just a few more steps, and then she saw her: Rachel, right there where the sensor said she would be, crouched next to the guitar case, her body language a study in tension.

That's when a flicker of movement caught Alex's attention off to her left.

She stopped, squinted. There it was again—something moving in the small office. It was black, metallic . . .

Her eyes ticked over a few degrees to the right, to an equipment locker tucked between two metal support beams flush against one wall. She saw the same kind of movement there, and then again a few yards farther into the hangar, beside a huge spool of cable. It took a few seconds to realize what she was seeing, and when she did, Alex came very close to outright panic.

They were mercenaries, wearing the same style of body armor and holding the same kinds of weapons as the ones in the sublevels of the Steinholz Museum. They were all over the hangar . . . but they hadn't bothered Rachel yet.

That meant they were waiting.

Waiting to capture the BGO extraction team when they arrived, probably.

Waiting for *Alex*, so they could strap her to a table somewhere and vivisect her? Definitely.

She filled her lungs with air to scream a warning, but then a shadow rocketed in from one side and knocked all the breath from her body. She hit the ground hard, her head bouncing off the pavement.

Stars swarmed in front of her eyes as someone jerked her off the ground. Her jellied knees wouldn't hold her up, but that didn't matter because the arm clamped across her throat did the trick just fine. Alex managed a weak, thready gasp, before the person holding her began dragging her away.

Even without seeing him, she knew who it was: Sabre Cromwell. She recognized the scent of his breath. He didn't say anything as he hauled her away, out of Rachel's line of sight— and Rachel still hadn't noticed her.

Cromwell dragged Alex toward the one airplane parked on the field: the small, private jet. Its entry stairway had been lowered, and Alex's feet left the ground completely as he pulled her swiftly up into the plane.

The increased pressure of Cromwell's forearm on her trachea choked Alex very nearly into unconsciousness. When Cromwell threw her down in the passenger cabin, Alex could only lie there for a few moments, not moving, her face pressed into the expensive plush carpeting. Dully, she watched as Cromwell pulled up the lightweight stairs, then sealed and latched the plane's doorway. He turned and looked down at her. Dark red light from the setting sun painted his face; he looked like he was wearing a demonic mask.

"Right bit of luck you had, girl." He knelt and slipped the sensor off of her wrist and tossed it away. "But that's over now." Alex groaned and rolled onto her side, weakly trying to get up. Cromwell watched her dispassionately. "Enjoy the flight. It's the last bit of comfort you're going to get."

He stood and moved forward, disappearing into the cockpit. The door closed behind him, and for a few seconds Alex thought she was alone.

Then a voice spoke out from behind her in elegant British English, with a few recognizable touches of a Russian accent.

"Ingenious devices, those sensors you wear."

Alex struggled to a sitting position and turned her head. Sonnet Ivandrova perched in a nearby seat, watching her with a predatory expression. She twirled Alex's sensor around one finger. "I have made sure the one your friend wears shall be of no consequence." The sensor began to glow and shimmer, then to *smoke*. "Just as I do now with this one." As Alex watched, the device melted, drops of liquefied metal dripping down onto the carpet. "But I have to wonder . . . why is it calibrated to one-half of your miles? What significance does that distance hold?"

Alex didn't move, didn't say anything. *That shimmer! That was just like when I send the Alex Primes back!*

The idea that Sonnet Ivandrova might use the same kind of power she did completely derailed any other train of thought.

The older woman seemed to find Alex's stunned silence amusing. "Oh, do not worry. The question was rhetorical. At least as far as you are concerned." She leaned forward and fixed Alex with a steely gaze. "You will answer me . . . when I wish you to."

At that moment the plane shuddered with the vibration of the engines starting up.

chapter twenty-five

From her "hiding" place, down behind a stack of crates in the hangar, Rachel heard the plane's engines start to rev. She had no idea what to do. She'd thought the plane was empty.

For the last twenty minutes she'd been crouched there, feeling like a fool and worried sick, since her proximity sensor had overheated and fuzzed out thirty seconds after she'd reached the airfield. She knew Alex had to be close. Alex's signal, though erratic, had continued approaching and was only a tenth of a mile away the last time she checked.

But now Rachel felt stuck. This was the rendezvous, the place where she and Alex were to be picked up by BGO operatives . . . at some point. She was there, with the sword; Alex was on her way; circumstances seemed to be about as good as they were going to get, despite how creepy the abandoned field felt.

But now, with the plane she'd believed to be empty suddenly springing to life . . . should she go investigate? Should she wait for Alex? It wasn't as if she could just jog up to a jet airplane and knock on the door and say, "Would you mind pulling over so I can ask you a few questions?" Besides, the plane's pilot seemed eager to get off the ground. It was already taxiing, about to take off.

Rachel stayed where she was, waiting.

* * *

On the plane, her face all but pressed against a window, Alex was beyond desperate. Within seconds they'd be airborne, and the half-mile safety zone would immediately vanish. The plane accelerated for takeoff.

Sonnet Ivandrova practically purred when she spoke. "You may as well sit down, miss. We have a long flight ahead of us, and Sabre was correct. This *is* the last time you'll experience comfort for quite awhile."

Alex paid Sonnet no attention. Scenarios flashed through her head, but they all wound up the same way: Rachel caught sight of the SKAR commandos and ran, but was hampered by the guitar case, so they grabbed her and shot her.

SKAR got the sword.

Or maybe she fought and she beat them, but then Alex went out of range and Rachel disappeared, leaving the case behind.

SKAR got the sword.

Or, more likely, the ambush moved in on Rachel and twelve or fifteen guys shot her point-blank, and it wouldn't matter if Alex was out of range or not.

SKAR got the sword.

To her horror, Alex felt the landing gear leave the pavement. They were airborne, and all was lost.

She could see it playing out in her head: the Vosarak computer virus would take hold. The world's economy would collapse, throwing the whole planet into chaos. Any key figures that might have rallied people or led some kind of resistance would get zombified and rendered useless or dead. Then SKAR's sleeper agents would all activate, and *they* would become the leaders, unifying country after country, all of them reporting to the three insane ghouls who shared SKAR's throne.

Alex's life to this point hadn't been much to talk about, really. Compared with other girls her age, she'd experienced virtually nothing. She'd grown up in what amounted to an orphanage. Never once had she opened a Christmas present or received a birthday card from anyone called Mom or Dad.

But she cherished the things she *had* experienced. She cherished her friends, Gail and Chuck. She cherished B.C. She even cherished Second-in-Command. And if the sword didn't get back to the Square to be decoded, all of that would vanish—*replaced* with a world designed by three nutcases who belonged in an asylum.

Hot tears burned Alex's eyes. She looked around the cabin, desperate . . . and then she noticed something. The setting sun's light shone through the plane's windows, casting red squares on the opposite wall of the cabin. And as Alex watched, those squares slid from the wall right up onto the ceiling.

The plane was banking. Sharply.

Alex blinked back her tears and turned to face Sonnet. "You think there's nothing I can do right now, don't you? You think there's no way you could fail."

Sonnet grinned smugly. "It *would* be a bit difficult for you to leave our company at this point."

Alex narrowed her eyes, her heart practically exploding in her chest. "Watch me."

She took one running step, drew back her undamaged fist, and punched Sonnet Ivandrova squarely in the nose as hard as she could. Something went *crunch*.

The blow had exactly the effect Alex had hoped it would. Well, she hadn't planned to break her good hand—and she was pretty sure that's what had just happened—but the crunching had come from Sonnet's nose. Sonnet howled in pain, her nostrils gushing blood, and within seconds both her eyes blackened.

"What the hell are you *doing?*" Sonnet wailed, but Alex didn't stop to reflect. She grabbed Sonnet, hauled her out of her seat, and threw her against the wall right next to the door, keeping her pinned with one elbow.

Then Alex popped the seals on the door, one after another. She'd been paying close attention to Sabre Cromwell as he fastened them before takeoff.

Sonnet didn't realize what Alex was up to at first, she was so distracted by the blood pouring out of her nose. But when Alex threw the last seal open, the truth dawned on her, and

Sonnet went into a frenzy. Struggling to get away from Alex, she thrashed and punched and kicked, spattering blood all over the cabin, but it was too little, too late.

Alex grabbed a good handful of Sonnet's coat and kicked the door open.

Sonnet shrieked like a banshee as the wind instantly swept them both out of the plane.

Air roared past as they plummeted, and Alex wrapped herself around Sonnet like an octopus. "You crazy little *bitch!*" Sonnet screamed. "You've killed us!"

"Oh, I don't think so!" Alex craned her neck and looked down at Kohler Air Field directly below them. The plane had circled, its flight path in the opposite direction from the runway. It had taken them right back over Rachel and the waiting SKAR commandos. "I think you've got more tricks than that!"

"You're insane!" Sonnet blasted back at her.

Alex grimaced. "Come on! *Quit stalling!*"

Sonnet snarled, her face suddenly ugly with hate and rage, but Alex's bet paid off. A shimmering heat wave effect suddenly enveloped Sonnet's entire body, much more strongly than before—and a parachute winked into existence, already deployed, anchored firmly to Sonnet's back by very solid-looking straps.

As the wind buoyed them up, the sudden jerking halt almost shook Alex loose, but she hung on, shrieking at the pain exploding in her injured wrist. Another glance down showed her that the airfield was still below them.

Then she looked Sonnet dead in the eye.

"Is this chute real? Or is it going to vanish if you get even crazier and decide you want to die after all?"

Sonnet's words were filled with venom. "It's as real as you are, you pitiful little troll."

Alex said, "Good," whipped her head back, and then brought her forehead down right between Sonnet's eyes. Sonnet went limp.

Clinging to the unconscious woman and her magically summoned parachute, Alex took a huge breath and screamed downward as loud as she could, *"Rachel! It's a trap! You're surrounded!"*

* * *

Rachel's head snapped up at the faint, familiar voice. She followed the sound, and witnessed a bizarre sight: floating down toward the nearest helipad, suspended from a huge dove-gray parachute, was a fat woman with two heads. Rachel realized what she was looking at a second later, just as Alex screamed again.

"It's a traaaaap!"

Galvanized, Rachel grabbed up the guitar case, spun around, and rushed headlong for the small office. The SKAR mercenaries, seeing that their ambush had been blown, came out of hiding and started shooting at her. Then one of them made an emphatic gesture at the others. In Italian he shouted, "Hold your fire! The Baron wants her alive!"

What he and the other mercenaries hadn't counted on was what Rachel had rushed into the office to get: something that she'd seen earlier, before settling into her hiding spot. Now she came back out, holding an implement that looked very comfortable in her grip.

A fire axe.

Rachel charged the nearest of the mercenaries and swung the axe, her teeth bared and her hair flying like some female barbarian on the cover of a fantasy novel. The man took the hit on his shoulder, and because he was wearing body armor, it didn't kill him. What the blow *did* do was break a couple of bones and knock him flat on the ground, senseless.

Rachel took a stand in the door of the office, her back to the guitar case she'd left inside. "Okay," she snarled. "Come on."

The mercenaries charged. Rachel met them, her axe flashing and flying. She dealt out a similar treatment to two more attackers, and then a fourth. She was like a one-woman demolition crew, smashing her way through the men.

As Alex and Sonnet touched down roughly fifty feet away, Rachel screamed and flew into an even greater frenzy, crushing and hacking until nine of the fifteen men lay prone around her, unconscious or in so much pain they were rendered worthless.

For a moment there was a standoff. A cold wind whistled across the pavement, lofting Rachel's hair about her head in an impressive, dramatic cloud. The fire axe glinted red in her hands. Then the remaining mercenaries decided on the most prudent course of action: they turned tail and ran, sprinting away out of sight around the hangar. Maybe five seconds passed before an engine roared to life and a brown van burned rubber out of there.

Alex got to her feet, standing next to the still-unconscious Sonnet Ivandrova. "Rachel? You okay?"

Rachel nodded and leaned on the axe for a second, catching her breath. "Hang on. I just need to get the sword." She turned toward the office—and stopped dead in her tracks. Alex followed Rachel's gaze and gasped.

Framed in the doorway, battered and bloody, stood David Yu. He held the guitar case in one hand and gripped the collar of an unconscious SKAR soldier in the other. He walked slowly over to Rachel, dragging the man behind him.

The three of them stood there for a long moment, Rachel and Alex both staring at David. No one spoke.

Then David grinned, let the mercenary drop to the pavement, and handed Rachel the guitar case. "I caught him trying to sneak out a window with this thing," he said casually. "And . . . y'know . . . much as I'd love to take it home with me . . . right now I think it's better off in your hands."

Alex was afraid to approach him. She knew as soon as she turned her back on Sonnet, the older woman would disappear somehow. So, staying where she was, she called out, "David? Are you hurt? What happened to you and Yvette?"

Rachel didn't know what to think about this little spectacle. She simply watched as David walked slowly over to Alex, limping noticeably.

"Cromwell got the better of us, obviously. Yvette's laid up for a while, but she'll be okay. I could still get around, so I came here first chance I got. Good thing I did, huh?"

Alex didn't think she'd ever seen a more attractive man in her entire life.

Just as she was about to speak, the sound of chopper blades reached them. Alex turned to look and saw an enormous helicopter in the distance, swiftly approaching the airfield.

"I'm sure that's your ride," David said. "I think I'll make myself scarce now."

"But . . ." Alex began.

"It's okay." He smiled; it looked a little lopsided since his lower lip was swollen. "I'll see you around."

Neither Alex nor Rachel made a move to stop him as he limped around the side of the hangar, out of sight.

Rachel came over to Alex, the guitar case with the sword in it held casually by her side. "You going to tell me what that was all about?" Her eyes twinkled.

"As soon as I figure it out myself, sure." She paused, grimacing as pain flared in her wrist again. "But I'll tell you one thing right now."

Rachel readied herself, unsure of what to expect . . . but Alex's next words were filled with nothing but admiration. "That was *incredible!* With that *axe?* My God! You were like some sort of superhero!"

Rachel grinned. "Well, y'know . . . it's not like I've never used a fire axe before."

Alex was about to continue, but just then the huge, dual-rotor helicopter came in for a landing.

The large side door opened up, and ten huge mute-suits jumped out. Alex's eyes widened a little to see that they were all armed with fully automatic machine pistols—and then her eyes got wider at the person stepping out of the aircraft behind them. It was Sec, all business.

She marched up to the two of them, her face grim. "You have the Vosarak Sword?"

Rachel patted the guitar case in answer. "Safe and sound."

Sec nodded once. Then she glanced down at the unconscious woman lying on the ground at their feet, and her face turned three entertaining shades of red and purple in rapid succession.

"I—that's—you—that's—"

Alex and Rachel grinned at each other.

"Yes, it is," Alex said. "She and Sabre Cromwell kidnapped me, but I punched her and pulled her out of an airplane and here we are. Plus, Rachel's a superhero."

Sec looked from Sonnet to Alex to Rachel and back again for a good twenty seconds. Then, to Alex's astonishment, she burst into tears, threw her arms wide and gave them both huge hugs.

"I was so *worried!*" Sec exclaimed, her voice overcome with emotion. Alex's astonishment grew more profound. "I thought you were both *dead!*"

While Alex was busy being speechless, two of the mute-suits hustled over and picked up Sonnet's limp body. Alex and

Rachel followed Sec back to the helicopter, just as Sec noticed Alex's wrist.

"Oh, Alex, you're hurt! Is that *broken?*" She barked an order at a mute-suit, "Hilinski! Get the first aid kit!"

"So . . . you're not mad?" Alex asked tentatively.

"Of course not."

Once they were belted in and lifting off, with Hilinski tending to her wrist, Alex asked, "Well . . . then . . . want to hear about the rest of the stuff we've done?"

Sec had regained her composure, and fixed Alex with an even gaze. For a moment, Alex thought Sec's emotional outburst had been a fluke never to be seen again, especially when Sec said, "Procedure dictates that all details be saved for the debriefing." But then her face practically split in half with a grin. "But who cares about procedure at a time like this? Tell me *everything!*"

Alex laughed the first truly relaxed laugh she'd had in quite awhile.

The helicopter rose to cruising altitude and headed west.

chapter twenty-six

Alex had expected that the welcome back and going away party was even more boisterous than usual this time. BGO missions didn't ordinarily go completely haywire, and when they did, they *never* came out this successfully. Rachel got mobbed by every male in the Bureau, but was very polite and gracious about the experience.

The two things Alex had not expected at the party came in quick succession.

First: she'd thought that at least *someone* would congratulate her in the same way they were congratulating Rachel. After all, she *had* been directly responsible for the mission's success. Partly, anyway.

But no. The attention fell squarely on Rachel. Hardly anyone gave Alex even a second glance, except Rachel herself, who caught Alex's eye from over a short guy's head. Rachel stood in the middle of the conference room, standard protocol, while Alex hovered near the bar, also standard. But then Rachel motioned with her head for Alex to join her.

That was a first.

Not fully sure of exactly why she did it, Alex smiled, made a declining gesture with her splinted left hand, and mouthed the words, "Nah, you go ahead." She could tell that confused Rachel, but then Matthew broke their line of sight as he moved in for another one of his schmooze-fests.

Still smiling, Alex slipped out the side door into the hallway, a cup of ginger ale in her right hand.

Then the second thing she didn't expect to see walked around a corner and spoke to her. B.C. looked normal, expression solemn, suit perfect, but his voice was even drier than usual when he said, "That was quite an experience for your first time out, wasn't it?"

Alex's smile widened, and she chuckled. "You're not kidding. So, will I be getting a raise now, or what?"

B.C.'s solemn expression darkened into a grim, black frown, and Alex's smile crumbled and died.

"We don't give raises to operatives who jeopardize their missions to pursue foolish personal agendas. You were sent over there to *talk* to people. Not to get into physical altercations. Not to engage in breaking-and-entering. Not to risk your life frivolously. Just to *talk*."

Wincing, Alex said, "Should we maybe go to your office for this?"

B.C. stepped closer. "You strayed so far afield from your stated objectives and parameters, it's a miracle the sword was recovered. Your actions have been called under review, young lady. Second-in-Command will advise you early next week as to what disciplinary actions will be taken."

Alex tried to keep her knees from trembling as B.C. paused, considering his next words. "*However.* Analysis of the sword, cross-referenced with the computer virus, has already led R&D a long way toward crafting a firewall. Proper measures should be in place within twenty-four hours."

"Well, that's . . . that's good, right?"

B.C. hadn't blinked the entire time he'd been standing there. Finally, he did. "Yes. That's good."

Without another word, he turned on his heel and walked away from her.

Alex watched him go. A bead of condensation from her ginger ale dropped onto her foot.

Then Rachel came out into the hallway and shut the door behind her. "Alex—you okay? You've got a funny look on your face."

"Y'know . . . nah. I'm good. How are you? Anxious to get back home?"

Rachel ran a hand over her hair. "I am, yeah. I know Donal must be wondering what the hell happened to me. But I've got to say . . . I'm really going to miss you."

Alex smiled. "Seriously?"

"Well *yeah.*" Rachel glanced over her shoulder at the conference room door. "And another thing! I mean it, it is *so* wrong that you're not getting any credit around here for what *we* did."

Alex shrugged. "All these people have known me my whole life. They just always think of me sitting in the back of a van while people like you do all the hard work. Plus, with all the communications weirdness going on, they might not even know about what all happened."

Rachel folded her arms. "Well then, someone should *tell* them."

Alex threw her cup into a nearby trashcan, then leaned against the wall near Rachel and shoved her hands in her pockets. She felt very comfortable around her other self. "Y'know what I've been thinking about?"

"What's that?"

"The conversation we had here, in the wardrobe room, before we left for Paris. What you said about knowing something that nobody else knows—and how that can make you powerful."

"Right . . . ?"

"I'm starting to think my life is like that. I can do this *incredible* thing . . . So nobody knows about it, and I don't get any credit for it. But, y'know, so what? I'm thinking maybe it's *my* secret. Not theirs. And it's making *me* powerful."

Rachel's eyes twinkled. "So you're considering basing your life philosophy around a comment I made about lacy underwear."

Alex burst out giggling. "Well . . . yeah, pretty much, I guess so."

Rachel put her arm around Alex's shoulders, and the two of them started toward the elevator.

Alex said, "I *do* wish you could stay around long enough to show me how to get my hair to behave like yours."

"That's easy enough. It's just a matter of the right product."

"For real? Tell me! Wait, let me get something to write this down . . ."

The two young women chatted casually on their way down to the lower level. Alex ran back over everything they'd been through in so short a time: Paris, the zombies, Berlin . . . two of the three heads of SKAR! She got a mini adrenaline rush just thinking about it.

The elevator doors opened, letting them out into the laboratory complex. Rachel glanced around, then looked Alex in the eye. "So this is it, huh?"

Alex nodded. It was hard to smile. "Last week, if somebody said to me, 'You're really going to miss the next Alex Prime once she's gone,' I would've called him a liar to his face."

Rachel laughed and pulled Alex to her in a gentle hug, minding her wrist. "Wish I had you for a kid sister."

They separated. Tears collected in Alex's eyes, but she smiled a genuine smile. "Hope I can grow up and be as cool as you."

"You're already grown up, Alex." Then, she said teasingly, "Now you've just got to work on the 'cool' part."

Alex mimicked outrage, then laughed through her tears. "Thank you."

Rachel took a step backward. Ready. She winked. "Don't mention it."

Then Alex closed her eyes . . . and Rachel vanished in a sparkling cloud of lights.

* * *

Ninety minutes later, Alex opened the door to her condo and walked inside, looking around as if she'd never seen it before. Her luggage from the trip stood stacked neatly beside her bedroom door, delivered earlier from the Square. *That's the BGO for you. Service with anonymity.*

From his cage, Worsel the parrot screeched, "Bonkers! Bonkers! Bonkers!" Alex strolled over to him. He pressed his beak against the cage's bars. She rubbed it affectionately.

"Bonkers? What the hell have the Bureau guys been saying to you?"

With his eyes closed in pleasure, Worsel said, "Alex. Best friends."

Alex chuckled, feeling peaceful. She went to the phone and dialed Gail and Chuck's number.

Gail answered, "Hi!" just as sprightly as ever.

"Hey, I'm back," Alex said. "You guys busy? Ready to cash in a pizza-and-movie rain check?"

"Oh, jeez, I'm *really* sorry," Gail said, and Alex believed her. "But we *have* to study tonight."

"Okay—that's cool. I'll talk to you later."

Alex hung up the phone and discovered to her small, pleasant surprise, that it *was* cool. She was awfully tired, and her recliner looked pretty inviting. Maybe socializing for the evening was a little beyond her, after all.

In the bedroom, Alex shoved her suitcase up onto her bed and opened it, intending to take out only what she needed for that night. The major unpacking could wait.

She frowned. The clothes in her case looked so *drab*. Old and drab and boring.

Picking up a sweater, she murmured, "Goodwill for you, shopping for me." She was about to start making a pile in the corner when a tiny, folded scrap of paper fell out of the sweater and drifted down to the bedspread.

Puzzled, not recognizing the scrap, Alex picked it up and unfolded it.

As she read it, her face went through a unique series of expressions. Then she jumped up on the bed and hopped up and down and then got back down and danced out into the living room, all to the tune of imaginary but very dramatic music.

Written on the paper in very neat, masculine script were the words: *I meant everything I told you*, followed by: *Next time you're in Paris*, and then a phone number. It was signed, *David*.

Alex looked around for someplace safe to put the scrap of paper, saw nothing satisfactory, and finally tucked it into her bra. She couldn't seem to stop grinning. Her face was in danger of cramping, but still she couldn't stop.

With a light, bouncy step, Alex went to the dartboard and pulled the darts out of their various resting places. She went back to the line of tape on the floor, turned, said, "Next time I'm in Paris," and hurled a dart.

With a very satisfying *thunk,* the dart sank perfectly into the center of the tiny red bull's-eye.

epilogue

A two hundred-year-old crystal goblet shattered explosively into slivers and dust against the enormous stone fireplace's back wall.

Baron Giacomo Morbidini, standing five feet to the fireplace's left, his hand resting lightly on the back of an antique chair worth several tens of thousands of dollars, didn't move or change expression in the slightest. When he spoke, the tone of his rumbling voice was mild. "I only have so many of those, Sabre."

Sabre Cromwell, trembling in the middle of the Baron's parlor, clenched his fists convulsively, relaxed them, then clenched them again. Veins in his temple and throat stood out sharply, bulging slightly with each rapid beat of his heart.

"Alex Benno made a fool out of me," he ground out. "Now the sword is lost, Sonnet is lost . . . all I could do was keep going! Just fly off and leave her there. With *them*. If only you'd have let me make more drones—"

"No! They are too difficult to control, too high profile. I've told you that before. I don't like using them." The Baron's eyes narrowed. "Are you questioning my orders?"

"No, sir." Cromwell's shoulders sagged.

"Besides, Sonnet will be fine." The Baron lifted a similar crystal goblet to his lips and sipped a thick, dark liquid that would have killed anyone else. "You act as if she were defenseless."

Cromwell paced angrily. "I know she'll be fine. I just don't want her there, imprisoned. She—" He caught himself, as if realizing he was about to say too much, but then said it anyway in a very soft voice. "She deserves to be free."

The Baron finished his drink and moved closer, towering over Cromwell. "Freedom is a relative thing. For all we know, Sonnet may be enjoying her stay at the Square. There are certainly enough familiar faces there for her to feel at home."

Cromwell grunted in acknowledgment. The Baron strode past him and opened the parlor door. "Come along, Sabre. If it's the BGO you want to focus on, let us focus on a much more productive facet of it."

"You mean Alex Benno?"

"The very one. Now that we know her name . . . we are free to set about bringing her over to our way of thinking."

"Or silencing her permanently."

The Baron dipped his head. "We shall see."

Baron Morbidini walked out of the room, and Cromwell followed him, the cruel smile resurfacing on his lips.

TO BE CONTINUED IN BOOK TWO:
ALEX UNLIMITED: SPLIT-SECOND SIGHT

COSMOgirl!

Be Your Own Hero

Article by Kierna Mayo

Illustration by Al-Insan Lashley

be your own hero

Put away the red cape, Supergirl! You can inspire bold acts of greatness—*in yourself*. And we promise you won't have to leap a single tall building! By Kierna Mayo

Christina Aguilera has an amazing voice. Sofia Coppola cracked the Hollywood boys' club and proved she's got a powerful director's eye. Maybe you look up to Even Ensler for her work to stop violence against women, or you're in awe of Pat Tillman, the NFL star who left fame and fortune to fight in Afghanistan—and lost his life this spring. They're all heroes. But here's the thing: Christina sometimes can't hit the high notes, Sofia has days when she's in a creative slump, Eve's struggle may sometimes feel overwhelming to her, and even Pat might have had fears about going to war. Each of them has had unsure, insecure, *unheroic* moments, just like you. So if these heroes are like you, who's to say you can't be like *them?* You can. In fact, they'll *help* you become a brave girl who can overcome any hurdle life puts in her way. You can be a hero in your own live—here's how.

get to the core

The first step is to make a list of people you look up to on the chart below. Don't censor yourself if someone seems like a silly choice. It's your list, and no one else has to see it. It can include people you know (like your mom or a favorite aunt), celebrities you think are cool, public figures who made history (like Sally Ride, the first American woman in space), or even fictional characters (Hermione Granger is no pushover!) Then ask yourself what you admire about them. Let's say you pick Beyoncé Knowles: The first quality of hers you might come up with is poise—after all, she never seems annoyed, no matter how many photographers are in her face. Next, try to break that down to an even deeper value—her poise probably comes from self-confidence. When you drill down to the core values your heroes represent, it helps you see the qualities you want in yourself.

HERO →	VALUE →	CORE VALUE!
Beyoncé	poise	self-confidence

create your own dream team

Take another look at your list, and then fantasize that together those people make up your imaginary team of "Hero Allies"—a dream team of friends for every circumstance. Imagine that they are always with you—literally, like sitting next to you on the bus or standing next to your computer at home. (Okay, so that's a bit kooky, but go with it.) This way you can ask them for help at any time. It doesn't matter if these are people you'll never meet; what counts is that you can claim their strengths as your own.

Suppose you have a friend who's smoking a lot of weed and it makes you uncomfortable. You could easily stand by, quietly thinking to yourself a million times how much you hate it. *Or* you could tap the courage that one of your Allies gives you and decide to tell your friend how concerned you are about her. When you talk to her, you may discover that she is glad you cared enough to bring it up and she wants to share her honest feelings with you. And with that one simple action, you've helped her *and* yourself. Or maybe you're struggling in a class. It might feel like you're admitting a weakness to ask the girl who's getting straight A's to tutor you. *But what would Beyoncé do?* Someone with as much drive as Beyoncé might say that it's more important to do whatever it takes to succeed than to avoid action in order to protect your pride. Listen to her. Because that's what being your own hero is about—following your inner spirit with a little inspiration from your Allies.

the bottom line

So where do you go from here? By choosing your heroes and identifying the values that you cherish most, you're saying to yourself and the world, "These are my ground rules. This is how I operate." With that as your road map, and an inspirational crew as your guides, hard decisions about school, guys, friends—*whatever*—will start to be a little easier. You might find that at first, you call on your Allies a lot. But over time, their values will start to feel more and more a part of you. And that's when you'll have truly become your own personal hero.

aLex unLimited

COVER CONCEPT SKETCHES

BY JARED BOONE

Here Alex looks pretty young. She's slouching and ankle-deep in snow to show her awkwardness and discomfort. Behind her are some of her alternates—a scientist, a spy, an athlete, and a surfer girl. This is the first time I worked with snow to illustrate the summoning of an Alex Prime.

I didn't
want Alex
to be an ugly
duckling, but
she is a bit of a
wallflower, always
uncomfortable
in her own skin.
I drew her hair
unkempt—frizzy
but not so out-
of-control that it
dominated the
picture. I wanted
to capture the
feeling of being
dwarfed, closed
off, and a tad
overwhelmed.

We aimed for a more sophisticated and mature approach in this draft. I cropped out her eyes to experiment with an "Everywoman" approach. Here I used snow people in the background to signify Alex's alternates. I didn't want the duplicates to look like clones, so I tried to make them all slightly different.

The snow people evolved to have more definition. I was going to give them all props to differentiate their personalities, but decided to go for a more uniform look. I took Alex out of the chair so she wasn't so imposing. To represent the idea of individuality, I placed snowflakes in the background, hoping it wouldn't clutter the design.

aLex unLimited

COVER CONCEPT: PHOTO REALISTIC

BY ANNE MARIE HORNE

We decided to go with a photorealistic cover, and our model Sara Shapley
totally fit the bill. She encapsulated Alex's vulnerability, sarcastic edge, natural
poise, free spirit, and endless potential. The photo shoot was lots of fun and
we got hundreds of excellent pictures. Choosing just one was very difficult.

We did a series
of headshots. This one shows Alex
looking young, a little unsure—definitely a wallflower.
But there's an underlying grace there, too. Something about her
makes you want to get to know her better.

We put Sara in various outfits to shoot Alex's alternates. Here she's got a kind of geeky-schoolmarm thing going on.

This is a sporty Alex Prime. I like the shape of the hood and hair framing her face—it really draws the focus right to her expressive eyes. it was neat to see how a few simple changes in outfit and hairstyle could drastically alter the look, feel, and mood of the character.

This is "scary-militant-ninja" Alex, as we like to call her. The Alex Primes are usually older and more sophisticated; in this photo, Alex really has a dark edge. You don't want to mess with this prime.

Here's a relaxed, random pose we thought about using later in the series, as Alex's confidence and sense of self develops.

Ultimately, we decided to go with a close up for the cover, but we got some lovely portrait shots. Here Alex is in one of her classic frumpy sweaters, a bitter-sweet smile signaling her mixed feelings about her government gig. Alex Benno is an ordinary girl with extraordinary talents, and I think that concept really makes this book so special!

Check out the following series also available from TOKYOPOP Fiction:

www.tokyopop.com/popfiction

POP
FICTION